TOM SWIF[illegible]

AIR SCOUT

OR

Uncle Sam's Mastery of the Sky

By

VICTOR APPLETON

NEW WEST PRESS

ISBN 978-1-64965-137-2

New West Press
Henderson, NV 89052
www.nwwst com

Ordering Information:
Special discounts are available on quantity purchases by corporations, associations, educators, and others. For details, contact the publisher at the listed address below.

U.S. trade bookstores and wholesalers: Please contact New West Press:

Tel: (480) 648-1061; or email: contact@nwwst.com

CONTENTS

"LOOK! LOOK!" EXCLAIMED TOM. "DOESN'T THAT SEEM SUSPICIOUS?"

CHAPTER I

A SKY RIDE

"Oh Tom, is it really safe?"

A young lady—an exceedingly pretty young lady, she could be called—stood with one small, gloved hand on the outstretched wing of an aeroplane, and looked up at a young man, attired in a leather, fur-lined suit, who sat in the cockpit of the machine just above her.

"Safe, Mary?" repeated the pilot, as he reached in under the hood of the craft to make sure about one of the controls. "Why, you ought to know by this time that I wouldn't go up if it wasn't safe!"

"Oh, yes, I know, Tom. It may be all right for you, but I've never been up in this kind of airship before, and I want to know if it's safe for me."

The young man leaned over the edge of the padded cockpit, and clasped in his rather grimy hand the neatly gloved one of the young lady. And though the glove was new, and fitted the hand perfectly, there was no attempt to withdraw it. Instead, the young lady seemed to be very glad indeed that her hand was in such safe keeping.

"Mary!" exclaimed the young man, "if it wasn't safe—as safe as a church—I wouldn't dream of taking you up!" and at the mention of "church" Mary Nestor blushed just the least bit. Or perhaps it was that the prospective excitement of the moment caused the blood to surge into her cheeks. Have it as you will.

"Come, Mary! you're not going to back out the last minute, are you?" asked Tom Swift. "Everything is all right. I've made a trial flight, and you've seen me come down as safely as a bird. You promised to go up with me. I won't go very high if you don't like it, but my experience has been that, once you're off the ground, it doesn't make any difference how high you go. You'll find it very fascinating. So skip along to the house, and Mrs. Baggert will help you get into your togs."

"Shall I have to wear all those things—such as you have on?" asked Mary, blushing again.

"Well, you'll be more comfortable in a fur-lined leather suit," asserted Tom. "And if it does make you look like an Eskimo, why I'm sure it will be very becoming. Not that you don't look nice now," he hastened to assure Miss Nestor, "but an aviation suit will be very—well, fetching, I should say."

"If I could be sure it would 'fetch' me back safe, Tom—"

"That'll do! That'll do!" laughed the young aviator. "One joke like that is enough in a morning. It was pretty good, though. Now go on in and tog up."

"You're sure it's safe, Tom?"

"Positive! Trot along now. I want to fix a wire and—"

"Oh, is anything broken?" and the girl, who had started away from the aeroplane, turned back again.

"No, not broken. It's only a little auxiliary dingus I put on to make it easier to read the barograph, but I think I'll go back to the old system. Nothing to do with flying at all, except to tell how high up one is."

"That's just what I don't care to know, Tom," said Mary Nestor, with a smile. "If I could imagine I was sailing along only about ten feet in the air I wouldn't mind so much."

"Flying at that height would be the worst sort of danger. You leave it to me, Mary. I won't take you up above the clouds on this sky ride; though, later, I'm sure you'll want to try that. This is only a little flight. You've been promising long enough to take a trip with me, and now I believe you're trying to back out."

"No, really I'm not, Tom! Only, at the last minute, the machine looks so small and frail, and the sky is so—big—"

She glanced up and seemed to shiver just a trifle.

"Don't be thinking of those things, Mary!" laughed Tom Swift. "Trot along and get ready. The motor never worked better, and we may break a few speed records this morning. No traffic cops to stop us, either, as there might be if we were in an auto."

"There you go, Mary!" exclaimed Tom, as if struck with a new thought. "You've ridden in an auto with me many a time, and you never were a bit afraid, though we were in more danger than we'll be this morning."

"Danger, Tom, in an auto? How?"

"Why, danger of a wheel collapsing as we were going full speed; or the steering knuckle breaking and sending us into a tree; danger of running into a stone wall or a ditch; danger of some one running into us, or of us running into some one else. There isn't one of these dangers on a sky ride."

"No," said Mary slowly. "But there's the danger of falling."

"One against twenty. That's the safety margin. And, if we do fall, it will be like landing in a feather bed! There, don't wait any longer. Go and get ready."

Mary sighed, and then, seeming to summon her nerve to her aid, she smiled brightly, waved her hand to Tom, and hastened toward his home, where Mrs. Baggert the matronly housekeeper, was waiting to help the girl attire herself in a flying-suit of leather.

Mary Nestor, who had a very warm place in the heart of

Tom Swift, had, as he stated, some time since promised to take a trip in the air with the young inventor. But she had kept putting it off, for one reason or another, until Tom began to despair of ever getting her to accompany him. To-day, however, when she had called to inquire about his father, who had been slightly ill, Tom had, after the social visit, insisted on the promise being kept.

He had his mechanic get out one of the safest, though a speedy, double machine, and, with Mary to watch, Tom had taken a trial flight, just to show her how easy it was. It was not the first time she had seen him take to the air, but now she watched with different emotions, for she was vitally interested.

Tom had sailed down from aloft, making a landing in the aviation field he had constructed near his home, and then he had insisted that Mary should keep her promise to take a sky ride with him.

"Don't be too long now!" called Tom to the girl, as she hurried toward the house. "Never mind about your hair, or whether your hat's on straight. You're going to wear a cap, anyhow, and tuck your hair up under that. It's hot down here, but it will be cold up above; so tell Mrs. Baggert to see that you're warmly dressed."

"All right," and gaily she waved her hand to him. Now that she had made her decision, and was really going up, she was not half so frightened as she had been in the contemplation of it.

As Tom climbed out of the machine, to give it a careful inspection, though he was certain there was nothing wrong, an aged colored man shuffled toward him.

"Yo'—yo'll be mighty careful ob Miss Nestor now, won't yo', Massa Tom?" asked the man.

"Of course I will, Eradicate," was the young inventor's answer.

"Case we ain't got many laik her no mo', an' dat's de truf, Massa Tom," went on the old man. "So be mighty careful laik!"

"That's what I will, Rad! And, while I'm up in the air, don't you and Koku have any trouble."

"Ho! Trouble wif dat onery no-'count giant! I guess not!" and the colored man limped off, highly indignant.

Satisfied, from an inspection of his machine, that it was as nearly mechanically perfect as it was possible to be, Tom Swift finished his trip around it and stood near the big propeller, waiting for Mary Nestor to reappear. Presently she did so, and Tom gaily waved his hand to her.

"You're a picture!" he cried, as he saw how particularly "fetching" she looked in the aviator's costume which was like his own. Because of the danger of entanglement, Miss Nestor had doffed her skirts, and wore the costume of all aviators—men and women.

"I wish I had my camera!" cried Tom. "You look—stunning!"

"I hope that isn't any comment on how I'm going to feel if we have to make a—forced landing, I believe you call it," she retorted.

"Oh, I'll take care of that!" exclaimed Tom. "Now up you go, and we'll start," and he helped her to climb into the padded seat of the cockpit, behind where he was to sit.

"Oh, Tom! Don't be in such a hurry!" expostulated Mary. "Let me get my breath!"

"No!" laughed the young inventor. "If I did you might back out. Get in, fasten the strap around you and sit still. That's all you have to do. Don't be afraid, I'll be very careful. And don't try to yell at me to go slower or lower once we're up in the air.

"Why not?" Mary wanted to know, as she settled herself in her seat.

"Because I can't very well hear you, or talk to you. The motor makes so much noise, you know. We can do a little talking through this speaking tube," and he indicated one, "but it isn't very satisfactory. So if you have anything to say—"

"In the language of the poets," interrupted Mary, "if I have words to spill, prepare to spill them now. Well, I haven't! Now I'm here, go ahead! I shall probably be too frightened to talk, anyhow."

"Oh, no you won't—after the first little sensation," Tom assured her. "You'll be crazy about it. Come on, Jackson!" he called to the mechanician. "Start the ball rolling!"

Tom was in his place, his goggles and cap well down over his face, and he was adjusting the switch as the mechanic prepared to spin the propellers.

Suddenly a man came running from the Swift house, waving his arms not unlike the blades of an aircraft propeller, he also shouted, but Tom, whose ears were covered with his fur cap, could not hear. However, Jackson did, and stopped whirling the blades, turning about to see what was wanted.

"Why, it's Mr. Damon!" exclaimed Tom, as he caught sight of the excited man. "Hello, what's the matter?" the youth asked, pulling aside one flap of his head-covering so he might hear the answer.

"Tom! Wait a minute! Bless my mouse trap!" exclaimed Mr. Damon, "I want to speak to you!" He was panting from his run across the field. "I just got to your house—saw your father—he said you were going up with Miss Nestor, but—bless my dog biscuit—"

"Can't stop now, Mr. Damon!" answered Tom, with a laugh. "I have only just succeeded, by hard work, in getting Mary to a point where she has consented to take a sky ride. If I stop now she'll back out and I'll never get her in again. See you when I come back," and Tom pulled the covering over his ear once more.

"But, Tom, bless my shoe laces! This is important!"

"So's this!" answered Tom, with a grin. He saw, by the motion of Mr. Damon's lips, what the latter had said.

Around swung the propeller blades. The gasoline vapor in the cylinders was being compressed.

"Contact!" called Tom sharply, as he pressed the switch to give the igniting spark at the proper moment. The mechanic had stepped back out of the way, in case there should be a premature starting of the powerful engine, in which event the blades would have cut him to pieces.

"Wait, Tom! Wait! This is very important! Bless my collar button, Tom Swift, but this is—"

Bang! Bang! Bang!

With a series of explosions, like those of a machine gun, the motor started, and further talk was out of the question. Tom turned on more gas. The propellers became almost invisible blades of light and shadow, and the aeroplane began moving over the grassy field. The mechanic had sprung out of the way, pulling Mr. Damon with him.

"Come back! Come back! Wait a minute, Tom Swift! Bless my pansy blossoms, I want to tell you something!" cried the little man.

But Tom Swift was away and out of hearing. He had started on his sky ride with Mary Nestor.

CHAPTER II

A NEW IDEA

Any one who has taken a flight in an aeroplane or gone up in a balloon, will know exactly how Mary Nestor felt on this, her first sky ride of any distance. For a moment, as she looked over the side of the machine, she had a distinct impression, not that she was going up, but that some one had pulled the earth down from beneath her and, at the same time, given her a shove off into space. Such is the first sensation of going aloft. Then the rush of air all about her, the slightly swaying motion of the craft, and the vibration caused by the motor took her attention. But the sensation of the earth dropping away from beneath her remained with Mary for some time.

This sensation is much greater in a balloon than in an aeroplane, for a balloon, unless there is a strong wind blowing, goes straight up, while an aeroplane ascends on a long slant, and always into the teeth of the wind, to take advantage of its lifting power on the underside of the planes. The reason for this sensation—that of the earth's dropping down, instead of one's feeling, what really happens, that one is ascending—is because there are no objects by which comparison can be made. If one starts off on the earth's surface at slow, or at great speed, one passes stationary objects—houses, posts, trees, and the like—and judges the speed by the rapidity with which these are left behind.

Going up is unlike this. There is nothing to pass. One simply cleaves the air, and only as it rushes past can one be sure of movement. And as the air is void of color and form, there is no sensation of passing anything.

So Mary Nestor, as she shot into the air with Tom Swift, had a sensation as though the earth were dropping from beneath her. For a moment she felt as though she were in some vast void—floating in space—and she had a great fear. Then she calmed herself. She looked at Tom sitting in front of her. Of course, all she could see was his back, but it looked to be a very sturdy back, indeed, and he sat there in the aircraft as calmly as though in a chair on the ground. Then Mary took courage, and ceased to grasp the sides of the cockpit with a grip that stiffened all her muscles. She was beginning to "find herself."

On and on, and up and up, went Mary and Tom, in this the girl's first big sky ride. The earth below seemed farther and farther away. The wide, green fields became little emerald squares, and the houses like those in a toy Noah's ark.

Down below, Mr. Wakefield Damon, who had hurried over from his home in Waterfield to see Tom Swift, gazed aloft at the fast disappearing aeroplane and its passengers.

"Bless my coal bin!" cried the eccentric man, "but Tom is in a hurry this morning. Too bad he couldn't have stopped and spoken to me. It might have been greatly to his advantage. But I suppose I shall have to wait."

"You want to see Master?" asked a voice behind Mr. Damon, and, turning, he beheld a veritable giant.

"Yes, Koku, I did," Mr. Damon answered, and he did not appear at all surprised at the sight of the towering form beside him. "I wanted to see Tom most particularly. But I shall have to wait. I'll go in and talk to Mr. Swift."

"Yaas, an' I go talk to Radicate," said the giant. "Him diggin' up ground where Master told me to make garden. Radicate not strong enough for dat!"

"Huh! there's trouble as soon as those two get to disputing," mused Mr. Damon, as he went toward the house.

Meanwhile, Mary was beginning to enjoy herself. The sensation of moving rapidly through the air in a machine as skillfully guided as was the one piloted by Tom Swift was delightful. Up and up they went, and then suddenly Mary felt a lurch, and the plane, which was now about a thousand feet high, seemed to slip to one side.

Mary screamed, and began reaching for the buckle of the safety belt that fastened her to her seat. She saw that something unusual had occurred, for Tom was working frantically at the mechanism in front of him.

But, in spite of this, he seemed aware that Mary was in danger, not so much, perhaps, from what might happen to the machine, as what she might do in her terror.

"Oh! Oh!" cried the girl, and Tom heard her above the terrific noise of the motor, for she was speaking with her lips close to the tube that served as a sort of inter-communicating telephone for the craft. "Oh, we are falling! I'm going to jump!"

"Sit still! Sit still for your life!" cried Tom Swift. "I'll save you all right! Only sit still! Don't jump!"

Mary, her red cheeks white, sank back, and the young inventor redoubled his efforts at the controls and other mechanisms.

And that Tom was perfectly qualified to make a safe landing, even with engine trouble, Mary Nestor well knew. Those of you who have read the previous books of this series know it also, but, for the benefit of my new readers, I shall state that this was by no means Tom's first ride in an aeroplane.

He had operated and built gasoline engines ever since he was about sixteen years old. As related in the initial volume of this series, entitled, "Tom Swift and His Motorcycle," he became possessed of this machine after it had started to climb a tree with Mr. Damon on board. After that experience the eccentric man—blessing everything he could think of—had no liking for the speedy motorcycle and sold it to Tom at a low price.

That was the beginning of a friendship between the two, and also started Tom on his career as an inventor and a possessor of many gasoline craft. For he was not content with merely riding the repaired motorcycle. He made improvements on it.

Tom lived with his father in the town of Shopton, their home being looked after, since the death of Mrs. Swift, by Mrs. Baggert. Mr. Wakefield Damon lived in the neighboring town of Waterfield, and spent much time at Tom's home, often going on trips with him in various vehicles of the land, sea or air.

As related in the various volumes of this series, Tom was not content to remain on earth. He built a speedy motor boat, and then secured an airship, following that with a submarine. He also made an electric runabout that was the speediest car on the road. Sending wireless messages, having thrilling experiences among the diamond makers, journeying to the caves of ice, and making perilous trips in his sky racer took up part of the young inventor's time.

With his electric rifle he did some wonderful shooting, and in the "City of Gold" made some strange discoveries, part of the fortune he secured enabling him to build his sky racer. It was in a land of giants that Tom was made captive, but he succeeded in escaping, and brought two giants, of whom Koku was one, away with him.

Following this achievement Tom invented a wizard camera and a great searchlight, which, with his giant cannon, was purchased by the United States Government. Work on his phototelephone and his aerial warship, the problem of digging a big tunnel, and then traveling to the land of wonders, kept Tom Swift very busy, and he had just completed a wonderful piece of work when the present story opens.

This last achievement was the perfecting of a machine to aid in the great World War and you will find the details set down in the volume which immediately precedes this. "Tom Swift and His War Tank," it is called, and in that is related how he not only invented a marvelous machine, but succeeded in keeping its secret from the plotters who tried to take it from him. In this Tom was helped by the inspiration of Mary Nestor, whom he hoped some day to marry, and by Ned Newton, a chum, who, though no inventor himself, could admire one.

Ned and Tom had been chums a long while, but Ned inclined more to financial and office matters than to machinery. At times he had managed affairs for Tom, and helped him finance projects. Ned was now an important bank official, and since the United States had entered the war had had charge of some Red Cross work, as well as Liberty Bond campaigns.

Somehow, as she sat there in the craft which seemed disabled, Mary Nestor could not help thinking of Tom's many activities, in some of which she had shared.

"Oh, if he falls now, and is killed!" she thought. "Oh, what will happen to us?"

"It's all right, Mary! Don't worry! It's all right!" cried Tom, through the speaking tube.

"What's that? I can't hear you very well!" she called back.

"No wonder, with the racket this motor is making," he answered. "Why can't something be done so you can talk in an aeroplane as well as in a balloon? That's an idea! If I could tell you what was the matter now you wouldn't be a bit frightened, for it isn't anything. But, as it is—"

"What are you saying, Tom? I can't hear you!" cried Mary, still much frightened.

"I say it's all right—don't get scared. And don't jump!" Tom shouted until his ears buzzed. "It's all nonsense—having a motor making so much noise one can't talk!" he went on, irritatedly.

A strange idea had come to the young inventor, but there was no time to think of it now. Mentally he registered a vow to take up this idea and work on it as soon as possible. But, just now, the aeroplane needed all his attention.

As he had told Mary, there was really nothing approaching any great danger. But it was rather an anxious moment. If Tom had been alone he would have thought little of it, but with Mary along he felt a double responsibility.

What had happened was that the craft had suddenly gone into an "air pocket" or partial vacuum, and there had been a sudden fall and a slide slip. In trying to stop this too quickly Tom had broken one of his controls, and he was busily engaged in putting an auxiliary one in place and trying to reassure Mary at the same time.

"But it's mighty hard trying to do that through a speaking tube with a motor making a noise like a boiler factory," mused the young inventor. Tom worked quickly and to good purpose. In a few moments, though to Mary they seemed like hours, the machine was again gliding along on a level keel, and Tom breathed more easily.

"And now for my great idea!" he told himself.

But it was some time before he could give his attention to that.

CHAPTER III

THE BIG OFFER

Working with all the skill he possessed, Tom had got the aeroplane in proper working order again. As has been said, the accident was a trivial one, and had he been alone, or with an experienced aviator, he would have thought little of it. Then, very likely, he would have volplaned to earth and made the repairs there. But he did not want to frighten Mary Nestor, so he fixed the control while gliding along, and made light of it. Thus his passenger was reassured.

"Are we all right?" asked Mary through the tube, as they sailed along.

"Right as a fiddle," answered Tom, shouting through the same means of communication.

"What's that about a riddle?" asked Mary, in surprise at his seeming flippancy at such a time.

"I didn't say anything about a riddle—I said we are as fit as a fiddle!" cried Tom. "Never mind. No use trying to talk with the racket this motor makes, and it isn't the noisiest of its kind, either. I'll tell you when we get down. Do you like it?"

"Yes, I like it better than I did at first," answered Mary, for she had managed to understand the last of Tom's questions. Then he sailed a little higher, circled about, and, a little later, not to get Mary too tired and anxious, he headed for his landing field.

"I'll take you home in the auto," he cried to his passenger. "We could go up to your house this way—in style—if there was a field near by large enough to land in. But there isn't. So it will have to be a plain, every-day auto."

"That's good enough for me," said Mary. "Though this trip is wonderful—glorious! I'll go again any time you ask me."

"Well, I'll ask you," said Tom. "And when I do maybe it won't be so hard to hold a conversation. It will be more like this," and he shut off the motor and began to glide gently down. The quiet succeeding the terrific noise of the motor exhaust was almost startling, and Tom and Mary could converse easily without using the tube.

Then followed the landing on the soft, springy turf, a little glide over the ground, and the machine came to a halt, while mechanics ran out of the hangar to take charge of it.

"I'll just go in and change these togs," said Mary, as she alighted and looked at her leather costume.

"No, don't," advised Tom. "You look swell in em. Keep 'em on. They're yours, and you'll need 'em when we go up again. Here comes the auto. I'll take you right home in it. Keep the aviation suit on.

"I wonder what Mr. Damon could have wanted," remarked Tom, as he drove Mary along the country road.

"He seemed very much excited," she replied.

"Oh, he almost always is that way—blessing everything he can think of. You know that. But this time it was different, I'll admit. I hope nothing is the matter. I might have stopped and spoken to him, but I was afraid if I did you'd back out and wouldn't come for a sky ride."

"Well, I might have. But now that I've had one, even with an accident thrown in, I'll go any time you ask me, Tom," and Mary smiled at the young inventor.

"Shucks, that wasn't a real accident!" he laughed. "But I do wonder what Mr. Damon wanted."

"Better go back and find out, Tom," advised Mary, as they stopped in front of her house.

"Oh, I want to come in and talk to you. Haven't had a chance for a good talk today, that motor made such a racket."

"No, go along now, but come back and see me this afternoon if you like."

"I do like, all right! And I suppose Mr. Damon will be fussing until he sees me. Well, glad you liked your first ride in the air, Mary—that is, the first one of any account," for Mary had been in an aeroplane before, though only up a little way—a sort of "grass-cutting stunt," Tom called it.

Waving farewell to the pretty girl, the young aviator turned the auto about and speeded for his home and the shops adjoining it. His father had not been well, of late, and Tom was a bit anxious about him.

"Mr. Damon may bother him, though he wouldn't mean to," thought Tom. "He seemed to have his mind filled with some new idea. I wonder if it is anything like mine? No, it couldn't be. Well, I'll soon find out," and, putting his foot on the accelerator, Tom sent the machine along at a pace that soon brought him within sight of his home.

"Is father all right?" he asked Mrs. Baggert, who was out on the front porch, as though waiting for him.

"Oh, yes, Tom, he's all right," the housekeeper answered.

"Is Mr. Damon with him?"

"No."

"He hasn't gone home, has he?"

"No, he's around somewhere. But some one else is with your father. Some visitors."

"Any relations?"

"No; strangers. They came to see you, and they're rather impatient. I came out to see if you were in sight. Your father sent me."

"Are they bothering him—talking business that I ought to attend to when he's ill? That mustn't be."

"Well, I suppose it is business that the strangers are talking over with your father, Tom," said Mrs. Baggert, "for I heard sums of money spoken of. But your father seems to be all right, only a trifle anxious that you should come."

"Well, I'm here now and I'll attend to things. Where are the strangers, and who are they?"

"I don't know," answered the housekeeper. "I never saw them before, but they're in the library with your father. Do you think they'll stay to dinner? If you do, I'll have Eradicate or Koku catch and kill a chicken."

"If you let one do it don't tell the other about it," said Tom with a laugh, "or you'll have a chicken race around the yard that will make the visitors sit up and take notice."

There was great rivalry between Eradicate Sampson, the aged colored man, and Koku, the giant, and they were continually disputing. Each one loved and served Tom in his own way, and there was jealousy between them. Koku, the giant Tom had brought with him from the land where the young inventor had been made captive, was a big, powerful man, and could do things the aged colored servant could not attempt. But "Rad," as he was often called, and his mule "Boomerang" had long been fixtures on the Swift homestead. But old age crept on apace with Eradicate, though he hated to admit it, and Koku did many things the colored man had formerly attended to, and Rad was always on the lookout not to be supplanted. Hence Tom's warning to Mrs. Baggert about letting the two be entrusted with the same mission of catching a chicken for the pot.

"Better get the fowl yourself and say nothing to either of them about it," Tom advised the housekeeper. "Mr. Damon will stay to dinner, as he always does when he comes, and as it's near twelve now, and as I may be delayed talking business to these strangers, you'd better get up a bigger meal than usual."

"I will, Tom," promised Mrs. Baggert. And then the young inventor, having seen that one of the men took the automobile to the garage, went into the house.

"Oh, here you are!" was his father's greeting, as he came out into the hall from the library. "I've been waiting anxiously for you, my boy. I couldn't think what was keeping you."

"Oh, I had a little trouble with the air machine—nothing serious."

A moment later Tom was standing before two well-dressed, prosperous-looking business men, who smiled pleasantly at him.

"Mr. Thomas Swift?" interrogated one, the elder, as he held out his hand.

"That's my name," answered Tom, pleasantly.

"I'm Peton Gale, and this gentleman is Boland Ware," went on the man who had taken Tom's hand. "I'm president and he's treasurer of the Universal Flying Machine Company, of New York."

"Oh, yes," said Tom, as he shook hands with Mr. Ware. "I have heard of your concern. You are doing a lot of government work, are you not?"

"Yes; war orders. And we're up to our neck in them. This war is going to be almost as much fought in the air as on the ground, Mr. Swift."

"I can well believe that," agreed Tom. "Won't you have a chair?"

"Well, we didn't come to stay long," said Mr. Gale with a laugh, which, somehow or other, grated on Tom and seemed to him insincere. "Our business is such a rushing one that we don't spend much time anywhere. To get down to brass tacks, we have come to see you to put a certain proposition before you, Mr. Swift. You are open to a business proposition, aren't you?"

"Oh, yes," answered Tom. "That's what I'm here for."

"I thought so. Well, now I'll tell you, in brief, what we want, and then Mr. Ware, our treasurer, can elaborate on it, and give you facts and figures about which I never bother myself. I attend to the executive end and leave the details to others," and again came that laugh which Tom did not like.

"You came here to make me an offer?" asked the young inventor, wondering to which of his many machines the visitors had reference.

"Yes," went on Mr. Gale, "we came here to make you a big offer. In short, Mr. Swift, we want you to work for our company, and we are willing to pay you ten thousand dollars a year for the benefit of your advice and your inventive abilities. Ten thousand dollars a year! Do you accept?"

CHAPTER IV

MR. DAMON'S WHIZZER

Characteristic it was of Tom Swift that he did not seem at all surprised at what most young men would call a liberal offer. Certainly not many youths of Tom's age would be sought out by a big manufacturing concern, and offered ten thousand dollars a year "right off the reel," as Ned Newton expressed it later. But Tom only smiled and shook his head in negation.

"What!" cried Mr. Gale, "you mean you won't accept our offer?"

"I can't," answered Tom.

"You can't!" exclaimed the treasurer, Mr. Ware. "Oh, I see. Mr. Gale, a word with you. Excuse us a moment," he added to Tom and his father.

The two men consulted in a corner of the library for a moment, and then, with smiles on their faces, once more turned toward the young inventor.

"Well, perhaps you are right, Tom Swift," said Mr. Gale. "Of course, we recognize your talents and ability, but you cannot blame us for trying to get talent, as well as material for our airships, in the cheapest market. But we are not hide-bound, nor sticklers for any set sum. We'll make that offer fifteen thousand dollars a year, if you will sign a five-year contract and agree that we shall have first claim on anything and everything you may patent or invent in that time. Now, how does that strike you? Fifteen thousand dollars a year—paid weekly if you wish, and our Mr. Ware, here, has a form of contract which can be fixed up and signed within ten minutes, if you agree."

"Well, I don't like to be disagreeable," said Tom with a smile; "but, really, as I said before, I can't accept your very kind offer. I may say liberal offer. I appreciate that."

"You can't accept!" cried Mr. Gale.

"Are you sure you don't mean 'won't'?" asked Mr. Ware, in a half growl.

"You may call it that if you like," replied Tom, a bit coolly, for he did not like the other's tone, "Only, as I say, I cannot accept. I have other plans."

"Oh, you—" began the brusk treasurer, but Mr. Gale, the president of the Universal Flying Machine Company, stopped his associate with a warning look.

"Just a moment, Mr. Swift," begged the president. "Don't be hasty. We are prepared to make you a last and final offer, and I do not believe you can refuse it."

"Well, I certainly will not refuse it without hearing it," said Tom, with a smile he meant to make good-natured. Yet, truth to tell, he did not at all like the two visitors. There was something about them that aroused his antagonism, and he said later that even if they had offered him a sum which he felt he ought not, in justice to himself and his father, refuse, he would have felt a distaste in working for a company represented by the twain.

"This is our offer," said Mr. Gale, and he spoke in a pompous manner which seemed to say: "If you don't take it, why, it will be the worse for you." He looked at his treasurer for a confirmatory nod and, receiving it, went on. "We are prepared to offer and pay you, and will enter into such a contract, with the stipulation about the inventions that I mentioned before—we are prepared to pay you—twenty thousand dollars a year! Now what do you say to that, Tom Swift?

"Twenty-thousand-dollars-a-year!" repeated Mr. Gale unctuously, rolling the words off his tongue. "Twen-ty-thou-sand-dol-lars-a-year! Think of it!"

"I am thinking of it," said Tom Swift gently, "and I thank you for your offer. It is, indeed, very generous. But I must give you the same answer. I cannot accept."

"Tom!" exclaimed his aged father.

"Mr. Swift!" exclaimed the two visitors.

Tom smiled and shook his head.

"Oh, I know very well what I am saying, and what I am turning down," he said. "But I simply cannot accept. I have other plans. I am sorry you have had your trip for nothing," he added to the visitors, "but, really, I must refuse."

"Is that your final answer?" asked Mr. Gale.

"Yes."

"Don't you want to take a day or two to think it over?" asked the treasurer. "Don't be hasty. Remember that very few young men can command that salary, and I may say you will find us liberal in other ways. You would have some time to yourself."

"That is what I most need," returned Tom. "Time to myself. No, thank you, gentlemen, I cannot accept."

"Be careful!" warned Mr. Gale, and it sounded as though there might be a threat in his voice. "This is our last offer, and your last chance. We will not renew this. If you do not accept our twenty thousand dollars now, you will never get it again."

"I realize that," said Tom, "and I am prepared to take the consequences.

"Very well, then," said Mr. Gale. "There seems nothing for us to do, Mr. Ware, but to go back to New York. I bid you good-day," and he bowed stiffly to Tom. "I hope you will not regret your refusal of our offer."

"I hope so myself," said Tom, lightly.

When the visitors had gone Mr. Swift turned toward his son, and, shaking his head, remarked:

"Of course, you know your own business best, Tom. Yet I cannot but feel you have made a mistake."

"How?" asked Tom. "By not taking that money? I can easily make that in a year, with an idea I have in mind for an improvement on an airship. And your new electric motor will soon be ready for the market. Besides, we don't really need the money."

"No, not now, Tom, but there is no telling when we may," said Mr. Swift, slowly. "This big war has made many changes, and things that brought us in a good income before, hardly sell at all, now."

"Oh, don't worry, Dad! We still have a few shots left in the locker—in other words, the bank. I'm expecting Ned Newton over any moment now, to give us the annual statement of our account, and then we'll know where we stand. I'm not afraid from the money end. Our business has done well, and it is going to do better. I have a new idea."

"That's all very well, Tom," said Mr. Swift, who seemed oppressed by something. "As you say, money isn't everything, and I know we shall always have enough to live on. But there is something about those two men I do not like. They were very angry at your refusal of their offer. I could see that. Tom, I don't want to be a croaker, but I think you'll have to watch out for those men. They're going to be your enemies—your rivals in the airship field," and Mr. Swift shook his head dolefully.

"Well, rivalry, when it's clean and above board, is the spice of trade and invention," returned Tom, lightly. "I'm not afraid of that."

"No, but it may be unfair and underhand," said Mr. Swift. "I think it would have been better, Tom, to have accepted their offer. Twenty thousand a year, clear money, is a good sum."

"Yes, but I may make twice that with something that occurred to me only a little while ago. Forget about those men, Dad, and I'll tell you my new idea. But wait, I want Mr. Damon to hear it, too. Where is he?"

"He was here a little while ago. He went out when those two men came and—"

At that moment, from the garden at the side of the library, the sound of voices in dispute could be heard.

"Now yo' all g'wan 'way from yeah!" exclaimed some one who could be none other than Eradicate Sampson. "Whut fo' yo' all want to clutter up dish yeah place fo'? Massa Tom said I was to do de garden wuk, an' I'se gwine to do it! G'wan 'way, Giant!"

"Ho! You want me to get out, s'pose you put me, black face!" cried a big voice, that of Koku, the giant.

"There they go! At it again!" cried Tom with a smile. "Might have known if I told Rad to do anything that Koku would be jealous. Well, I'll have to go out now and give that giant something to do that will tax his strength."

But as Tom was about to leave the room another voice was heard in the garden.

"Now, boys, be nice," said some one soothingly. "The garden is large enough for you both to work in. Rad, you begin at the lower end and spade toward the middle. Koku, you begin at the upper end and work down. Whoever gets to the middle first will win."

"Ha! Den I'll show dat giant some spade wuk as is spade wuk!" cried the colored man. "Garden wuk is mah middle name."

"Be careful, Rad!" laughed Mr. Damon, for he it was who was trying to act as peacemaker. "Remember that Koku is very strong."

"Yas, sah! He may be strong, but he's clumsy!" chuckled Eradicate. "You watch me beat him!"

"Ho! Black man get stuck in mud!" challenged Koku. "I show him!"

Then there was silence, and Tom and his father, looking out, saw the two disputants beginning to spade the soil while Mr. Damon, satisfied that he had, for the time being, stopped a quarrel, turned toward the house.

"I was just coming to look for you," said Tom. "Sorry I had to go off in such a hurry and leave you, but I had promised to take Mary for a ride, and as it was her first one, for a distance, I didn't want her to back out."

"That's all right, Tom, that's all right!" said Mr. Damon genially. "Ladies first every time. But I do want to see you, and it's about something important."

"No trouble, I hope?" queried Tom, for the manner of the eccentric man was rather grave.

"Trouble? Oh, no! Bless my frying pan, no trouble, Tom! In fact, it may be the other way about. Tom, I have an idea, and there may be millions in it! That's it—millions!"

"Good!" cried the young inventor. "Might as well bite off a big lump while you're at it. So you have a new idea! Well, I have myself, but I'll listen to yours first. What is it, Mr. Damon?"

"It's a new kind of airship, Tom. I haven't got it all worked out yet, but I can give you a rough outline. On my way over I got to thinking about balloons, aeroplanes and the like, and it occurred to me that the present principles are all wrong."

"So I evolved a new type of machine. I'm going to call it the Damon Whizzer. Maybe Demon Whizzer would be more appropriate, but we won't decide on that now. Anyhow, it's going to be a whizzer, and I want to talk to you about it. There is an entirely new principle of elevation and propulsion involved in my Whizzer, and I—"

At that moment there came a crash and clatter of steel and wood from the garden, out of sight of which Tom and Mr. Damon had walked while talking. Then followed a jangle of words.

"They're at it again!" cried Tom, as he ran toward the side of the house. "I guess it's a fight this time!"

CHAPTER V

TOM'S PROJECT

Curious was the sight that met the gaze of Tom Swift and Mr. Wakefield Damon as they rounded the corner of the house and looked into the newly spaded garden. There stood the giant, Koku, holding aloft in the air, by one hand, the form of the struggling colored man, Eradicate Sampson. And Eradicate was vainly trying to get at his enemy and rival, but was prevented by the long-distance hold the giant had on him.

"Yo' let me go, now! Yo' let me go, big man," cried Eradicate. "Ef yo' don't I'll bust yo' wide open, dat's whut I'll do! An' 'sides, I'll tell Massa Tom on yo', dat's whut I'll do!"

"Ho! You tell—I let you fall!" threatened Koku.

His threat was dire enough, for such was his size and strength that he held the colored man nearly nine feet from the ground, and a fall from that distance would seriously jar Eradicate, if it did nothing else. The colored man's eyes opened wide as he heard what Koku said, and then he cried:

"Let me down! Let me down, an' I won't say nuffin!"

"An' you let me scatter dirt?" asked Koku, for such was the giant's idea of working in the garden.

"Yes, yo' kin scatter de dirt seben ways from Sunday fo' all I keers!" conceded Eradicate. Then, as he was lowered to the ground, he and the giant turned and saw Mr. Damon and Tom approaching.

"What's wrong?" asked the young inventor.

"'Scuse me, Massa Tom," began Eradicate, "but didn't yo' tell me to spade de garden?"

"I guess I did," admitted Tom Swift.

"An' you tell me help—yes?" questioned Koku.

"Well, I thought it would be a little too much for you, Rad," said Tom, gently. "I thought perhaps you'd like help."

"Hu! Not him, anyhow!" declared the colored man in great disgust. "When I git so old dat I cain't spade a garden, den me an' Boomerang, we-all gwine to die, dat's all I got to say. I was a-spadin' my part ob de garden, Massa Tom, same laik Mr. Damon done tole me to, an' dish yeah big mess ob bones steps on my side ob de middle an—"

"Him too slow. Koku scatter dirt twice times so fast!" declared the giant, whose English was not much better than Eradicate's.

"Yes, I see," said Tom. "You are so strong, Koku, that you finished your part before Eradicate did. Well, it was good of you to want to help him."

At this the giant grinned at his rival.

"At the same time," went on Tom, winking an eye at Mr. Damon, "Eradicate knows a little more about garden work, on account of having done it so many years."

"Ha! Whut I tell yo', Giant!" boasted the colored man. It was his turn to smile.

"And so," went on Tom, judicially, "I guess I'll let Rad finish spading the garden, and you, Koku, can come and help me lift some heavy engine parts. Mr. Damon wants to explain something to me."

"Ha! Nothing what so heavy Koku not lift!" boasted the giant.

"Go on! Lift yo'se'f 'way from heah!" muttered Eradicate as he picked up his dropped spade. And then, with a smile of satisfaction, he fell to work in the mellow soil while Tom led Koku to one of the shops where he set him to lifting heavy motor parts about in order to get at a certain machine that was stored away in the back of one of the rooms.

"That will keep him busy," said the young inventor. "And now, Mr. Damon, I can listen to you. Do you really think you have a new idea in airships?"

"I really think so, Tom. My Whizzer is bound to revolutionize travel in the air. Let me tell you what I mean. Now cast your mind back. How many ways are now used to propel an airship or a dirigible balloon through the air? How many ways?"

"Two, as far as I know," said Tom. "At least there are only two that have proved to be practical."

"Exactly," said Mr. Damon. "One with the propeller, or propellers, in front, and that is the tractor type. The other has the propeller in the rear, and that is the pusher type. Both good as far as they go, but I have something better."

"What?" asked Tom with a smile.

"It's a Whizzer," said the eccentric man. "Bless my gold tooth! but that is the best name I can think of for it. And, really, the propeller I'm thinking of inventing does whiz around."

"But are you going to use a tractor or pusher type?" Tom wanted to know.

"It's a combination of both," answered Mr. Damon. "As it is now, Tom, you have to get an aeroplane in pretty speedy motion before it will rise from the ground, don't you?"

"Yes, of course. That's the principle on which an aeroplane rises and keeps aloft, by its speed in the air. As soon as that speed stops it begins to fall, or volplane, as we call it."

"Exactly. Now, instead of having to depend on the speed of the aeroplane for this, why not depend on the speed of the propeller—in other words, the whizzer?"

"Well, we do," said Tom, a bit puzzled as to what his friend was trying to get at. "If the propeller didn't move the airship wouldn't rise—that is, unless it's of the balloon type."

"What I mean," said Mr. Damon, "is to have an aeroplane that will move in the air the same as a boat moves in the water. You don't have to get the propeller of a boat racing around at the rate of a million revolutions a minute, more or less, before your boat will travel, do you? If the engine turns the screw, or propeller, just over say fifty times a minute you would get some motion of the boat, wouldn't you?"

"Why, yes, some," admitted Tom.

"And what causes it?" asked Mr. Damon, anticipating a triumph.

"The resistance of the water to the blades of the screw, or propeller," answered Tom.

"Exactly! And it's the resistance of the air to the blades of an airship propeller that sends the craft along, isn't it?"

"Yes. And because of the difference in density between air and water it becomes necessary to revolve an aeroplane propeller many times faster than a boat propeller. It's the density that makes the difference, Mr. Damon. If air were as dense as water we could have comparatively slow-moving motors and propellers and—"

"Ha! There you have it, Tom! And there is where my Whizzer —Wakefield Damon's Whizzer—is going to revolutionize air travel!" cried the eccentric man. "The difference in density! If air were as dense as water the problem would be solved. And I have solved it! I'm going to turn the trick, Tom! One more question. How can air be made as dense as water, Tom Swift?"

"Why, by condensation or compression, I suppose," was the rather slow answer. "You know they have condensed, or compressed, air until it is liquid. I've done it myself, as an experiment."

"That's it, Tom! That's it!" cried Mr. Damon in delight. "Compressed air will do the trick! Not compressed to a liquid, exactly, but almost so. I'm going to revolve the propellers of my new airship in compressed air, so dense that they will not have to have a speed of more than seven hundred revolutions a minute. What's that compared to the three to ten thousand revolutions of the propellers now used? The propellers of Damon's Whizzer will be of the pusher type, and will revolve in dense, compressed air, almost like water, and that will do away with high speed motors, with all their complications, and make traveling in the clouds as simple as taking out a little one-cylinder motor boat. How's that, Tom Swift? How's that for an idea?"

To Mr. Damon's disappointment, Tom was not enthusiastic. The young inventor gazed at his eccentric friend, and then said slowly:

"Well, that's all right in theory, but how is it going to work out in practice?"

"That's what I came to see you about, Tom," was the reply. "Bless my tall hat! but that's just why I hurried over here. I wanted to tell you when I saw you going off on a trip with Miss Nestor. That's my big idea—Damon's Whizzer—propellers revolving in compressed air like water. Isn't that great?"

"I'm sorry to shatter your air castle," said Tom; "but for the life of me I can't see how it will work. Of course, in theory, if you could revolve a big-bladed propeller in very dense, or in liquid, air, there would be more resistance than in the rarefied atmosphere of the upper regions. And, if this could be done, I grant you that you could use slower motors and smaller propeller blades—more like those of a motor boat. But how are you going to get the condensed air?"

"Make it!" said Mr. Damon promptly. "Air pumps are cheap.

Just carry one or two on board the aeroplane, and condense the air as you go along. That's a small detail that can easily be worked out. I leave that to you."

"I'd rather you wouldn't," said Tom. "That's the whole difficulty—compressing your air. Wait! I'll explain it to you."

Then the young inventor went into details. He told of the ponderous machinery needed to condense air to a form approximating water, and spoke of the terrible pressure exerted by the liquid atmosphere.

"Anything that you would gain by having a slow-speed motor and smaller propeller blades, would be lost by the ponderous air-condensing machinery you would need," Tom told Mr. Damon. "Besides, if you could surround your propellers with a strata of condensed air, it would create such terrible cold as to freeze the propeller blades and make them as brittle as glass.

"Why, I have taken a heavy piece of metal, dipped it into liquid air, and I could shatter the steel with a hammer as easily as a sheet of ice. The cold of liquid air is beyond belief.

"Attempts have been made to make motors run with liquid air, but they have not succeeded. To condense air and to carry it about so that propellers might revolve in it, would be out of the question."

"You think so, Tom?" asked Mr. Damon.

"I'm sure of it!"

"Oh, dear! That's too bad. Bless my overshoes, but I thought I had a new idea. Well, you ought to know. So Damon's Whizzer goes on the scrap heap before ever it's built. Well, we'll say no more about it. You ought to know best, Tom. I wasn't thinking of it so much for myself as for you. I thought you'd like some new idea to work on."

"Much obliged, Mr. Damon, but I have a new idea," said Tom.

"You have? What is it? Tell me—that is, if it isn't a secret," went on the eccentric man, as much delighted over Tom's new plan as he had been over his own Whizzer, doomed to failure so soon.

"It isn't a secret from you," said Tom. "I got the idea while I was riding with Mary. I wanted to talk to her—to tell her not to jump out when we had a little accident—but I had trouble making myself understood because of the noise of the motor."

"They do make a great racket," conceded Mr. Damon. "But I don't suppose anything can be done about it."

"I don't see why there can't!" exclaimed Tom. "And that's my new idea—to make a silent aircraft motor—perhaps silent propeller blades, though it's the motor that makes the most noise. And that's what I'm going to do—invent a silent aeroplane. Not because I want so much to talk when I take passengers up in the air, but I believe such a motor would be valuable, especially for scouting planes in war work. To go over the enemy's lines and not be heard would be valuable many times.

"And that's what I'm going to do—work on a silent motor for Uncle Sam. I've got the germ of an idea and now—"

"Excuse me," said a voice behind Mr. Damon and Tom, and, turning, the young inventor beheld the form of Mr. Peton Gale, president of the Universal Flying Machine Company.

CHAPTER VI

MAKING PLANS

Tom Swift had drawn pencil and paper from his pocket, and, as he and Mr. Damon were sitting on the steps of one of the shops, the young inventor was about to demonstrate by a drawing part of his new project, when the interruption came in the shape of one of the men who had, an hour before, made a business offer to Tom.

"Excuse me," went on Mr. Peton Gale, "but Mr. Ware and I got to talking it over on our way to the station—the matter of having you in our company, Mr. Swift—and we concluded that it was worth twenty-five thousand dollars a year for us to have you. So I came back—"

"It isn't of the slightest use, Mr. Gale, I assure you," said Tom, a bit heatedly, for he did not like the persistency of this man, nor did he like his coming on the factory grounds unannounced and in this secret manner. "I told you I could not accept your offer. It is not altogether a matter of money. My word was final."

"Oh very well, if you put it that way," said Mr. Gale stiffly, "of course there is nothing more to say. But I thought perhaps you did not consider we had offered you enough and—"

"Your offer is fair enough from a financial standpoint," said Tom; "but I simply cannot accept it. I have other plans. Jackson!" he called to one of his mechanics who was passing, "kindly see Mr. Gale to the gate, and then let me know how it was any one came in here without a permit."

"Yes, sir," said the mechanic, as he stood significantly waiting.

"There was no one at the gate when I came in," said Mr. Gale, and his manner was antagonizing. "I wanted to speak to you—to ask you to reconsider your offer—so I came back."

"It is against the rules to admit strangers to the shop grounds," said Tom. "Good-day!"

The president of the Universal Flying Machine Company did not respond, but there was a look on his face as he turned away that, had Tom seen it, might have caused him some uneasiness. But he did not see. Instead, he resumed his talk with Mr. Damon.

"Tom, your idea is most interesting," declared the eccentric man. "I hope you will be able to work it out!"

"I'm going to try," said the young inventor. "I hope that man—Mr. Gale—didn't hear anything of what I was saying. He sneaked up on us before I was aware any one was near but ourselves."

"I don't imagine he heard very much, Tom," said Mr. Damon. "He may have heard you mention a silent motor—"

"That's just what I wish he hadn't heard," broke in Tom. "That's the germ of the idea, and once it becomes known that I am working on that— Well, there's no use crying over spilled milk," and he smiled at the homely proverb. "I'll have to work in secret, once I've started."

"Do you think the government would use it, Tom?" asked his friend.

"I should think it would be glad to. Consider what a wonderful part airships are playing in the present war. It really is a struggle to see which will be the master of the sky—the Allies or the Germans—and, up to recently, the Huns had the advantage. Then the Allies, recognizing how vital it was, began to forge ahead, and now Uncle Sam with his troops under General Pershing is leading everything, or will lead shortly. We have been a bit slow with our aircraft production, but now we are booming along. Uncle Sam will soon have the mastery of the sky."

"I hope so," sighed Mr. Damon. "We must beat the Germans!"

Briefly, Tom spoke of what Pershing's men were doing with their aeroplanes in France, and mention was made of what the French and British had done prior to the entrance of the United States into the World War.

"While we were yet neutral, Americans had made gallant names for themselves flying for France, and with my silent motor they ought to do better," declared Tom.

"Is silence its chief recommendation?" asked Mr. Damon.

"Yes," replied Tom. "Or rather, it will be when I have it perfected. Aeroplane motors now are about as compact and speedy as they can be made. It is only the terrific noise that is a handicap. It is a handicap to the pilots and observers in the craft, as they cannot communicate except through a special speaking tube, and this is not always satisfactory or sure. Then, too, the noise of an airship proclaims its approach to the enemy, sometimes long before it can be seen.

"With a silent motor all this would be done away with. With my new craft, in case I can perfect it, the enemy's lines can be approached as silently as the Indians used to approach the log cabins of the white settlers. That will be its great advantage—not that conversation can be more easily carried on, for that is, after all, an unimportant detail. But to approach the enemy's lines in the silence of the night would be a distinct gain."

"I believe it would, Tom!" exclaimed Mr. Damon. "And I should think, too, that Uncle Sam would be glad to get such a motor," he added.

"Well, he'll have one to take if he wants it, if I can make my plans a success," declared Tom. "That is, unless those other fellows get ahead of me."

"What other fellows?" asked Mr. Damon.

"Gale, Ware and their crowd," was the answer. "I fancy they are provoked because I wouldn't agree to work for them, and now, that Gale overheard—as he must have—what I propose working on, they may try that game themselves."

"You mean try to turn out a silent motor?"

"Yes. It would be a big feather in their cap for their company, so far, hasn't been very successful on government orders. That's why they came to me, I guess."

"I shouldn't be surprised, Tom," conceded Mr. Damon. "Since the government accepted your giant cannon and your great searchlight, you have come into greater prominence than ever before. And those two things are a wonderful success."

"Yes," admitted Tom, modestly enough, "the big electric light seems to have been of some benefit on the European battle front, and though they haven't been able to make and transport as many of my giant cannons as I'd like to see over there, it is progressing, I understand."

And this is true. For the details of these two inventions of Tom Swift's I refer my readers to the books bearing those titles. Sufficient to state here that the government was using these two inventions, and there had been no necessity for commandeering them either, since Tom had freely offered them at the declaration of war with Germany.

"Well, since I can't help you with my 'Whizzer,'" said Mr. Damon, with a smile, "let me do what I can toward your silent motor, Tom. What are you going to call it?"

"Oh, I don't know—hadn't thought of a name. I guess 'Air Scout' would be as good as any. That's what it will be—a machine for silently scouting in the air. And now to get down to brass tacks, as the poet says, I believe I will—"

"Gentleman to see you, Mr. Swift," interrupted Jackson.

"Bless my penwiper!" cried Mr. Damon. "More visitors! I hope it isn't Gale or Ware come back to see what they can spy on!"

CHAPTER VII

A PROBLEM IN SOUND

Tom Swift looked up with a distinct appearance of being annoyed that was unusual with him, for he was, nearly always, good-natured. But the frown that had replaced the pleasant look on his face while he was talking to Mr. Damon about the projected new air scout was at once wiped away as he looked at the card Jackson held out to him.

"Bring him in right away!" he ordered. "He needn't have stood on that ceremony."

"Well, he said it was a business call," returned the mechanician with a cheerful grin, "and he said he wanted it done according to form. So he gave me his card to bring you."

"Who is it?" asked Mr. Damon, with the privilege of an old friend.

"It's Ned Newton," Tom answered; "though why he's putting on all this formality I can't fathom."

Jackson went back to the main gate and told the man on guard there to admit Ned, who had so formally sent in his card.

"Ah, Mr. Swift, I believe?" began the bank employee with that suave, formal air which usually precedes a business meeting.

"That is my name," said Tom, with a suppressed grin, and he spoke as stiffly as though to a perfect stranger.

"Mr. Tom Swift, the great inventor?" went on Ned.

"Yes."

"Ah, then I am at the right place. Just sign here, please, on the dotted line," and he held out a blank form, and a fountain pen to Tom, who took them half mechanically.

"Huh? What's the big idea, Ned?" asked the young inventor, unable longer to carry on the joke. "Is this a warrant for my arrest, or merely a testimonial to you. If it's the latter, and concerns your nerve, I'll gladly sign it."

"Well, it's something like that!" laughed Ned. "That's your application for another block of Liberty Bonds, Tom, and I want you, as a personal favor to me, as a business favor to the bank, and as your plain duty to Uncle Sam, to double your last subscription."

Tom looked at the sum Ned had filled in on the blank form, and uttered a slight whistle of surprise.

"That's all right now," said Ned, with the air of a professional salesman. "You can stand that and more, too. I'm letting you off easy. Why, I got Mary's father—Mr. Nestor—for twice what he took last time, and Mary herself—hard as she's working for the Red Cross—gave me a nice application. So it's up to you to—"

"Nuff said!" exclaimed Tom, sententiously, as he signed his name. "I may have to reconsider my recent refusal of the offer of the Universal Flying Machine Company, though, if I haven't money enough to meet this subscription, Ned."

"Oh, you'll meet it all right! Much obliged," and Ned folded the Liberty Bond subscription paper and put it in his pocket. "But did you turn down the offer from those people?"

"I did," answered Tom. "But how did you know about it, Ned?"

"First let me say that I'm glad you decided to have nothing to do with them. They're a rich firm, and have lots of money, but I wouldn't trust 'em, even if they have some government contracts. The way I happened to know they were likely to make you an offer is this," continued Ned Newton.

"They do business with one of the New York banks with which my bank—notice the accent on the my, Tom—is connected. The other day I happened to see some correspondence about you. These flying machine people asked our bank to find out certain things about you, and, as a matter of business, we had to give the information. Sort of a commercial agency report, you know, nothing unusual, and it isn't the first time it's been done since your business got so large. But that's how I happened to know these fellows contemplated dickering with you."

"Do you know Gale or Ware?" Tom asked.

"Not personally. But in a business way, Tom, I'd warn you to look out for them, as they're sharp dealers. They put one over on the government all right, and there may be some unpleasant publicity to it later. But they're putting up a big bluff, and pretending they can turn out a lot of flying machines for use in Europe. Why don't you get busy on that end of the game, Tom?"

"I know you've more than done your bit, with Liberty Bonds, subscriptions to the Y. M. C. A. and other war work, besides your war tank and other inventions. But you're such a shark on flying machines I should think you'd offer your factory to the government for the production of aeroplanes."

"I would in a minute, Ned, and you know it; but the fact of the matter is my shops aren't equipped for the production of anything in large numbers. We do mostly an experimenting business here, making only one or two of a certain machine. I have told the government officials they can have anything I've got, and you know they wouldn't let me enlist when I was working on the war tank."

"Yes, I remember that," said Ned. "You're no slacker! I wanted to shoulder a rifle, too, but they keep me at this Liberty Loan work. Well, Uncle Sam ought to know."

"That's what I say," agreed Tom, "and that's why I haven't gone to the front myself. And now, as it happens, I've got something else in mind that may help Uncle Sam."

"What is it?"

"A silent flying machine for scout work on the battle front," Tom told his friend, and then he gave a few details, such as those he had been telling Mr. Damon.

"Then I don't wonder you turned down the offer of the Universal people," remarked Ned, at the conclusion of the recital. "This will be a heap more help to the government, Tom, than working for those people, even at twenty-five thousand dollars a year. And if you get short, and can't meet your newest Liberty Bond payments, why, I guess the bank will stretch your credit a little."

"Thanks!" laughed Tom, "but I'll try not to ask them."

The friends talked together a little longer, and then Ned had to take his departure to solicit more subscriptions, while Mr. Damon went with him, the eccentric man saying he would go home to Waterfield.

"But, bless my overshoes, Tom!" he exclaimed, as he departed, "don't forget to let me know when you have your silent motor working. I want to see it."

"I'll let you know," was the promise given by the young inventor.

"And watch out for those Universal people," warned Ned. "I'm not telling you this as a bank official, for I'm not supposed to, but it's personal."

"I'll be on the watch," said Tom. And, as he went into his private workshop, he wondered why it was his father and Ned had both warned him not to trust Gale and Ware.

The next few days were busy ones for Tom Swift. Once he had made up his mind to go to work seriously on a silent motor, all else was put aside. He sent a note to Mary Nestor, telling her what he was going to do, and, asking her to say nothing about it, which, of course, Mary agreed to.

"Come and see me when you can," she sent back word, "but I know you won't have much chance when you're experimenting with your invention. And I shall be working so hard for the Red Cross that I sha'n't get much chance to entertain you. But the war can't last forever."

"No," agreed Tom with a sigh, as he put away her letter, "and thank goodness that it can't!"

The young inventor threw himself into the perplexing work of inventing a silent motor with all the fervor he had given to the production of his war tank, his giant cannon, his wonderful searchlight and other machines.

"And," mused Tom, as he sat at his work table with pencil and paper before him, "since this is a problem in acoustics, I had best begin I suppose by going back to first principles, and after determining what makes an aeroplane engine noisy, try to figure out how to make it quiet. Now as to the first, the principle causes of noise are—"

And at that instant there broke on Tom's ears a succession of discordant sounds which seemed to be a combination of an Indian's war whoop and a college student's yells at a football game.

"Now I wonder what that is!" mused the young inventor as he hastily arose. "Better solve that problem before I tackle the aeroplane motor."

CHAPTER VIII

THROUGH THE ROOF

Tom rushed from his private office, and when he reached the outer door he heard with more distinctness the sounds that had alarmed him. They seemed to come from a small building given over to electrical apparatus, and which, at the time, was not supposed to be in use. It had been Tom's workroom, so to speak, when he was developing his electric runabout and rifle, but of late he had not spent much time in it.

"Somebody's in there!" reflected the young inventor, as he heard yells coming from the open door of the place. "And if it isn't Koku and Eradicate I miss my guess! Wonder what they can be doing there."

He crossed the yard between his private office and the electrical shop in a few rapid strides, and, as he entered the latter place, he was greeted with a series of wild yells.

"Good volume of sound here, at all events," mused Tom. "Almost as much as my motor made when I was trying to talk to Mary. Hello there! What's going on? Is any one hurt? What's the matter?" he cried, for, at first, he could see no one in the dim light of the place. The interior was a maze of electrical apparatus.

"Who's here?" demanded Tom, as he advanced.

"Oh, Master! Come quick! Koku 'most dead an' no can let go!" was the cry.

"Yo' jest bet yo' cain't let go!" chimed in the voice of Eradicate. "I done knowed yo would git into trouble ef yo' come heah, an' I'se glad ob it! So I is!"

"What is it, Rad? What has happened to Koku?" cried Tom, running forward, for though no very powerful current could be turned on in the electrical shop at this period of unuse, there was enough to be very painful. "What is it, Rad?"

"Oh, dat big foolish giant, Koku, done got his se'f into trouble!" chuckled the colored man. "He done got holt ob one ob dem air contraptions, Massa Tom, an' he cain't let go! Ha! Ha! Golly! Look at him squirm!" and Rad laughed shrilly, which accounted for some of the sounds Tom had heard.

Then came yells of rage and pain from the giant, and they were so loud and vigorous, mingling with Eradicate's as they did, that it was no wonder Tom was startled. The sounds were heard in the other shops, and men came running out. But before then Tom had put an end to the trouble.

One look showed him what had happened. Just how or why Koku and Eradicate had entered the electrical shop Tom did not then stop to inquire. But he saw that the giant had grasped the handles of one of the electric machines, designed for charging Leyden jars used in Tom's experiments, and the powerful, though not dangerous, current had so paralyzed, temporarily, the muscles of the giant's hands and arms that he could not let go, and there he was, squirming, and not knowing how to turn off the current, and unable to ease himself, while Eradicate stood and laughed at him, fairly howling with delight.

"Ha! Guess yo' won't do no mo' spadin' in' Massa Tom's garden right away, big man!" taunted Eradicate.

"Be quiet, Rad!" ordered Tom, as he reached up and pulled out the switch, thus shutting off the current. "This isn't anything to laugh at."

"But he done look so funny, Massa Tom!" pleaded the colored man. "He done squirm laik—"

But Eradicate did not finish what he intended to say. Once free from the powerful current, the giant looked at his numb hands, and then, seeming to think that Eradicate was the cause of it all, he sprang at the colored man with a yell. But Eradicate did not stay to see what would happen. With a howl of terror, he raced out of the door, and, old and rheumatic as he was, he managed to gain the stable of his mule, Boomerang, over which he had his humble but comfortable quarters.

"Well, I guess he's safe for a while!" laughed Tom, as he saw the giant turn away, shaking his fist at the closed door, for Koku, big as he was, stood in mortal terror of the mule's heels.

Tom locked the door of the electrical shop and went back to his interrupted problem. From Jackson he learned that Koku and Eradicate had merely happened to stroll into the forbidden place, which had been left open by accident. There, it appeared, Koku had handled some of the machinery, ending by switching on the current of the machine the handles of which he later unsuspectingly picked up. Then he received a shock he long remembered, and for many days he believed Eradicate had been responsible for it, and there was more than the usual hostile feeling between the two. But Eradicate was innocent of that trick, at all events.

"Though," said Tom, telling his father about it later, "Rad would have turned on the current if he had known he could make trouble for Koku by it. I never saw their like for having disagreements!"

"Yes, but they are both devoted to you, Tom," said the aged inventor. "But what is this you hinted at—a silent motor you called it, I believe? Are you really serious in trying to invent one?"

"Yes, Dad, I am. I think there's a big field for an aeroplane that could travel along over the enemy's lines—particularly at night—and not be heard from below. Think of the scout work that could be done.

"Well, yes, it could be done if you could get a silent motor, or propellers that made no noise, Tom. But I don't believe it can be done."

"Well, maybe not, Dad. But I'm going to try!" and Tom, after a further talk with his father, began work in earnest on the big problem. That it was a big one Tom was not disposed to deny, and that it would be a valuable invention even his somewhat skeptical father admitted.

"How are you going to start, Tom?" asked Mr. Swift, several days after the big idea had come to the young man.

"I'm going to experiment a bit, at first. I've got a lot of old motors, that weren't speedy enough for any of my flying machines, and I'm going to make them over. If I spoil them the loss won't amount to anything, and if I succeed—well, maybe I can help out Uncle Sam a bit more."

As Tom had said he would do, he began at the very foundation, and studied the fundamental principles of sound.

"Sound," the young inventor told Ned Newton, in speaking about the problem, "is a sensation which is peculiar to the ear, though the vibrations caused by sound waves may be felt in many parts of the body. But the ear is the great receiver of sound."

"You aren't going to invent a sort of muffler for the ears, are you, Tom?" asked Ned. "That would be an easy way of solving the problem, but I doubt if you could get the Germans to wear your ear-tabs so they wouldn't hear the sound of the Allied aeroplanes."

"No, I'm not figuring on doing the trick that way," said Tom with a laugh. "I've really got to cut down the sound of the motor and the propeller blades, so a person, listening with all his ears, won't hear any noise, unless he's within a few feet of the plane."

"Well, I can tell you, right off the reel, how to do it," said the bank employee.

"How?" asked Tom eagerly.

"Run your engine and propellers in a vacuum," was the prompt reply.

"Hum!" said Tom, musingly. "Yes, that would be a simple way out, and I'll do it, if you'll tell me how to breathe in a vacuum."

"Oh, I didn't agree to do that," laughed Ned.

But he had spoken the truth, as those who have studied physics well know. There must be an atmosphere for the transmission of sound, which is the reason all is cold and silent and still at the moon. There is no atmosphere there. Sound implies vibration. Something, such as liquid, gas, or solid, must be set in motion to produce sound, and for the purpose of science the air we breathe may be considered a gas, being composed of two.

Not only must the object, either solid, liquid, or gaseous, be in motion to produce sound, but the air surrounding the vibrating body must also be moving in unison with it. And lastly there must be some medium of receiving the sound waves—the ear or some part of the body. Totally deaf persons may be made aware of sound through the vibrations received through their hands or feet. They receive, of course, only the more intense, or largest, sound waves, and can not hear notes of music nor spoken words, though they may feel the vibration when a piano is played. And, as Ned has said, no sound is produced in a vacuum.

"But," said Tom, "since I can't run my aeroplane in a vacuum, or even have the propellers revolve in one, it's up to me to solve the problem some other way. The propellers don't really make noise enough to worry about when they're high in the air. It's the exhaust from the motor, and to get rid of that will be my first attempt."

"Can it be done?" asked Ned.

"I don't know," was Tom's frank answer.

"They do it on an automobile to a great extent," went on Ned. "Some of 'em you cant hardly hear."

"Yes, but an aeroplane engine runs many, many times faster than the motor of an auto," said Tom, "and there are more explosions to muffle. I doubt if the muffler of an auto would cut down the sound of an aero engine to any appreciable extent. But, of course, I'll try along those lines."

"They have mufflers or silencers for guns and rifles," went on Ned. "Couldn't you make a big one of those contraptions and put it on an aeroplane?"

"I doubt it," said Tom, shaking his head. "Of course it's the same principle as that in an auto muffler, or on a motor boat—a series of baffle plates arranged within a hollow cylinder. But all such devices cut down power, and I don't want to do that. However, I'm going to solve the problem or—bust!"

And Tom came near "busting," Ned remarked later, when he and his friend talked over the progress of the invention.

Two weeks had passed since the start of his evolution of his new idea, and following the visiting of the representatives of the Universal Flying Machine Company. Since then neither Gale nor Ware had communicated with Tom.

"But I must be on the watch against them," thought the young inventor. "I'm pretty sure Gale heard me mention what I was going to try to invent, and he may get ahead of me, and put a silent motor on the market first. Not that I'm afraid of being done out of any profits, but I simply don't want to be beaten."

The details of Tom's invention cannot be gone into, but, roughly, it was based on the principle of not only a muffler but also of producing less noise when the charges of gasoline exploded in the cylinders. It is, of course, the explosion of gasoline mixed with air that causes an internal combustion engine to operate. And it is the expulsion of the burned gases that causes the exhaust and makes the noise that is heard.

Tom was working along the well-known line of the rate of travel of sound, which progresses at the rate of about 1090 feet a second when air is at the freezing point. And, roughly, with every degree increase in the atmosphere's temperature the velocity of sound increases by one foot. Thus at a temperature of 100 degrees Fahrenheit, or 68 degrees above freezing, there would be added to the 1090 feet the 68 feet, making sound travel at 100 degrees Fahrenheit about 1158 feet a second.

Tom had set up in his shop a powerful, but not very speedy, old aeroplane engine, and had attached to it the device he hoped would help him toward solving his problem of cutting down the noise. He had had some success with it, and, after days and nights of labor, he invited his father and Ned, as well as Mr. Damon, over to see what he hoped would be a final experiment.

His visitors had assembled in the shop, and Eradicate was setting out some refreshments which Tom had provided, the colored man being in his element now.

"What's all this figuring, Tom?" asked Mr. Damon, as he saw a series of calculations on some sheets of paper lying on Tom's desk.

"That's where I worked out how much faster sound traveled

in hydrogen gas than in the ordinary atmosphere," was the answer. "It goes about four times as fast, or nearly four thousand two hundred feet a second. You remember the rule, I suppose. 'The speed of sonorous vibrations through gases varies inversely as the squares of the weights of equal volumes of the gases,' or, in other words—"

"Give it to us chiefly in 'other words,' if you please, Tom!" pleaded Ned, with a laugh. "Let that go and do some tricks. Start the engine and let's see if we can hear it."

"Oh, you can hear it all right," said Tom, as he approached the motor, which was mounted on a testing block. "The thing isn't perfected yet, but I hope to have it soon. Rad! Where is that black rascal? Oh, there you are! Come here, Rad!"

"Yaas sah, Massa Tom! Is I gwine to help yo' all in dish yeah job?"

"Yes. Just take hold of this lever, and when I say so pull it as hard as you can."

"Dat's whut I will, Massa Tom. Golly! ef dat no 'count giant was heah now he'd see he ain't de only one whut's got muscle. I'll pull good an' hard, Massa Tom."

"Yes, that's what I want you to. Now I guess we're all ready. Can you see, Dad—and Ned and Mr. Damon?"

"Yes," they answered. They stood near the side wall of the shop, while Tom and Eradicate were at the testing block, on which the motor, with the noise-eliminating devices attached, had been temporarily mounted.

"All ready," called the young inventor, as he turned on the gas and threw over the electrical switch. "All ready! Pull the starting lever, Rad, and when it's been running a little I'll throw on the silencer and you can see the difference."

The motor began to hum, and there was a deafening roar, just as there always is when the engine of an aeroplane starts. It was as though half a dozen automobile engines were being run with the mufflers cut out.

"Now I'll show you the difference!" yelled Tom, though such was the noise that not a word could be heard. "This shows you what my silencer will do."

Tom pulled another lever. There was at once a cessation of the deafening racket, though it was not altogether ended. Then, after a moment or two, there suddenly came a roar as though a blast had been let off in the shop.

Tom and Eradicate were tossed backward, head over heels, as though by the giant hands of Koku himself, and Mr. Damon, Ned, and Tom's father saw the motor fly from the testing block and shoot through the roof of the building with a rending, crashing, and splintering sound that could be heard for a mile.

CHAPTER IX

AFTER A SPY

Curious as it may seem, Eradicate, the oldest and certainly not the most energetic of the party assembled in the experiment room, was the first to recover himself and arise. Tottering to his feet he gave one look at the testing block, whence the motor had torn itself. Then he looked at the prostrate figures around him, none of them hurt, but all stunned and very much startled. Then the gaze of Eradicate traveled to the hole in the roof. It was a gaping, ragged hole, for the motor was heavy and the roof of flimsy material. And then the colored man exclaimed:

"Good land ob massy! Did I do dat?"

His tone was one of such startled contrition, and so tragic, that Tom Swift, rueful as he felt over the failure of his experiment and the danger they had all been in, could not help laughing.

"I take it, hearing that from you, Tom, that we're all right," said Ned Newton, as he recovered himself and brushed some dirt off his coat. Ned was a natty dresser.

"Yes, we seem to be all right," replied Tom slowly. "I can't say what damage the flying motor has done outside, but—"

"Bless my insurance policy! but what happened?" asked Mr. Damon. "I saw Eradicate pull on that lever as you told him to, Tom, and then things all went topsy-turvy! Did he pull the wrong handle?"

"No, it wasn't Rad's fault at all," said Tom. "The trouble was, as I guess I'll find when I investigate, that I put too much power into the motor, and the muffler didn't give any chance for the accumulated exhaust gases to expand and escape. I didn't allow for that, and they simply backed up, compressed and exploded. I guess that's the whole explanation."

"I'm inclined to agree with you, Son," said Mr. Swift dryly. "Don't try to get rid of all the noise at once. Eliminate it by degrees and it will be safer."

"I guess so," agreed Tom.

By this time a score of workmen from the other shops had congregated around the one though the roof of which the motor had been blown. Tom opened the door to assure Jackson and the others that no one was hurt, and then the young inventor saw the exploded motor had buried in the dirt a short distance away from the experiment building.

"Lucky none of us were standing over it when it went up," said Tom, as he made an inspection of the broken machine. "We'd have gone through the roof with it."

"She certainly went sailing!" commented Ned. "Must have been a lot of power there, Tom."

And this was evidenced by the bent and twisted rods that had held the motor to the testing block, and by the cylinders, some of which were torn apart as though made of paper instead of heavy steel. But for the fact that all the force of the explosion was directly upward, instead of at the sides, none might have been left alive in the shop. All had escaped most fortunately, and they realized this.

"Well," queried Ned, as Tom gave orders to have the damaged machine removed and the roof repaired, "does this end the wonderful silent motor, Tom?"

"End it! What do you mean—"

"I mean are you going to experiment any further?"

"Why, of course! Just because I've had one failure doesn't mean that I'm going to give up. Especially when I know what the matter was—not leaving any vent for the escaping gases. Why this isn't anything. When I was perfecting my giant cannon I was nearly blown up more than once, and you remember how we got stuck in the submarine."

"I should say I did!" exclaimed Ned with a shudder. "I don't want any more of that. But as between being blown through a roof and held at the bottom of the sea, I don't know that there's much choice."

"Well, perhaps not," agreed Tom. "But as for ending my experiments, I wouldn't dream of such a thing! Why, I've only just begun! I'll have a silent motor yet!"

"And a non-explosive one, I hope," added Mr. Damon dryly. "Bless my shoe buttons, Tom, but if my wife knew what danger I'd been in she'd never let me come over to see you any more."

"Well, the next time I invite you to a test I'll be more careful," promised the young inventor.

"There isn't going to be any next time as far as I'm concerned!" laughed Ned. "I think it's safer to sell Liberty Bonds."

And, though they joked about it, they all realized the narrow escape they had had. As for Eradicate, once he knew he had not been the one who caused the damage, he felt rather proud of the part he had taken in the mishap, and for many days he boasted about it to Koku.

True to his determination, Tom Swift did not give up his experimental work on the silent motor. The machine that had been blown through the roof was useless now, and it was sent to the scrap heap, after as much of it as possible had been salvaged. Then Tom got another piece of apparatus out of his store room and began all over again.

He worked along the same lines as at first—providing a chamber for the escaping gases of the exhaust to expend their noise and energy in, at the same time laboring to cut down the concussion of the explosions in the cylinder without reducing their force any. And that it was no easy problem to do either of these, Tom had to admit as he progressed. All previous types of mufflers or silencers had to be discarded and a new one evolved.

"Jackson, I need some one to help me," said Tom to his chief mechanician one day. "Haven't you a good man who is used to experimental work that you can let me take from the works?"

"Why, yes," was the answer. "Let me see. Roberts is busy on the new bomb you got up, but I could take him off that—"

"No, don't!" interposed Tom. "I want that work to go on. Isn't there some one else you can let me have?"

"Well, there's a new man who came to me well recommended. I took him on last week, and he's a wonderful mechanic. Knows a lot about gas engines. I could let you have him—Bower his name is. The only thing about it, though, is that I don't like to give you a man of whom I am not dead certain, when you're working on a new device."

"Oh, that will be all right," said Tom. "There won't be any secrets he can get, if you mean you think he might be up to spy work."

"That's what I did mean, Tom. You never can tell, you know, and you have some bitter enemies."

"Yes, but I'll take care this man doesn't see the plans, or any of my drawings. I only want some one to do the heavy assembling work on the experimental muffler I'm getting up. We can let him think it's for a new kind of automobile."

"Oh, then I guess it will be all right. I'll send Bower to you."

Tom rather liked the new workman, who seemed quiet and

efficient. He did not ask questions, either, about the machine on which he was engaged, but did as he was told. As Tom had said, he kept his plans and drawing under lock and key—in a safe to be exact—and he did not think they were in any danger from his new helper.

But Tom Swift held into altogether too slight regard the powers of those who were opposed to him. He did not appreciate the depths to which they would stoop to gain their ends.

He had been working hard on his new device, and had reached a point further along than when the other motor had exploded. He began to see success ahead of him, and he was jubilant. Whether this made him careless does not matter, but the fact was that he left Bower more to himself, and alone in the experimental shop several times.

And it was on one of these occasions, when Tom had been for some time in one of the other shops, where he and Jackson were in consultation over a new machine, that as he came back to the test room unexpectedly, he saw Bower move hastily away from in front of the safe. Moreover, Tom was almost certain he had heard the steel door clang shut as he approached the building.

And then, before he could ask his helper a question, Tom looked from a window and saw a stranger running hastily along the side of the building where his trial motor was being set up.

"Who's that? Who is that man? Did he come in here? Was he tampering with my safe?" cried Tom. He saw Bower hesitate and change color, and Tom knew it was time to act.

The window was open, and with one bound the young inventor was out and running after the stranger he had seen departing in such a hurry. The man was but a short distance ahead of him, and Tom saw he was stuffing some papers into his pocket.

"Here! Come back! Stop!" ordered Tom, but the man ran on the faster.

"That's a spy as sure as guns!" reflected Tom Swift. "And Bower is in with him!" he added. "I've got to catch that fellow!" and he speeded his pace as he ran after the fellow.

CHAPTER X

A BIG SPLASH

There was no question in the mind of Tom Swift but that the man he was running after was guilty of some wrong-doing. In the first place he was a stranger, and had no right inside the big fence that surrounded the Swift machine plant. Then, too, the very fact that he ran away was suspicious.

And this, coupled with the confusion on the part of Bower, and his proximity to the safe, made Tom fear that some of his plans had been stolen. These he was very anxious to recover if this strange man had them, and so he raced after him with all speed.

"Stop! Stop!" called Tom, but the on-racing stranger did not heed.

The cries of the young inventor soon attracted the attention of his men, and Jackson and some of the others came running from their various shops to give whatever aid was needed. But they were all too far away to give effective chase.

"Bower might have come with me if he had wanted to help," thought Tom. But a backward glance over his shoulder did not show that the new helper was engaging in the pursuit, and he could have started almost on the same terms as Tom himself.

The runaway, looking back to see how near the young inventor was to him, suddenly changed his course, and, noting this, Tom Swift thought:

"I've got him now! He'll be bogged if he runs that way," for the way led to a piece of swampy land that, after the recent rains, was a veritable bog which was dangerous for cattle at least; and more than one man had been caught there.

"He can't run across the swamp, that's sure," reflected Tom with some satisfaction. "I'll get him all right!"

But he wanted to capture the man, if possible, before he reached the bog, and, to this end, Tom increased his speed to such good end that presently, on the firm ground that bordered the swamp, Tom was almost within reaching distance of the stranger.

But the latter kept up running, and dodged and turned so that Tom could not lay hands on him. Suddenly, turning around a clump of trees the fleeing man headed straight for a veritable mud hole that lay directly in his path. It was part of the swamp—the most liquid part of the bog and a home of frogs and lizards.

Too late, the man, who was evidently unaware of the proximity of the swamp, saw his danger. His further flight was cut off by the mud hole, but it was too late to turn back. Tom Swift was at his heels now, and seeing that it was impossible to grab the man, Tom did the next best thing. He stuck out his foot and tripped him, and tripped him right on the edge of the mud hole, so that the man fell in with a big splash, the muddy water flying all around, some even over the young inventor.

For a moment the man disappeared completely beneath the surface, for the mud hole was rather deep just where Tom had thrown him. Then there was another violent agitation of the surface, and a very woebegone and muddy face was raised from the slough, followed by the rest of the figure of the man. Slowly he got to his feet, mud and water dripping from him. He cleared his face by rubbing his hands over it, not that it made his countenance clean, but it removed masses of mud from his eyes, nose, and mouth, so that he could see and speak, though his first operation was to gasp for breath.

"What—what are you doin'?" he demanded of Tom, and as the man opened his mouth to speak Tom was aware of a glitter, which disclosed the 'fact that the man had a large front tooth of gold.

"What am I doing?" repeated Tom. "I think it's up to you to answer that question, not me. What are you doing?"

"You—you tripped me into this mud hole!" declared the man.

"I did, yes; because you were trespassing on my property, and ran away instead of stopping when I told you to," went on Tom. "Who are you and what are you doing? What were you doing with Bower at my shop?"

"Nothin'! I wasn't doin' nothin'!"

"Well, we'll inquire into that. I want to see what you have in your pockets before I believe you. Come on out!"

"You haven't any right to go through my pockets!" blustered the stranger.

"Oh, haven't I? Well, I'm going to take the right. Jackson—Koku—just see that he doesn't get away. We'll take him back and search him," and Tom motioned to his chief machinist and the giant, who had reached the scene, to take charge of the man. But Koku was sufficient for this purpose, and the mud-bespattered stranger seemed to shrink as he saw the big creature approach him. There was no question of running away after that.

"Bring him along," ordered Tom, and Koku, taking a tight grip on the man by the slack of his garments behind, walked him along toward the office, the mud and water splashing and oozing from his shoes at every step.

"Now you look here!" the gold-toothed man cried, as he was

forced along, "you ain't got any right to detain me. I ain't done nothin'!" And each time he spoke the bright tooth in his mouth glittered in the sun.

"I don't know whether you've done anything or not," said Tom. "I'm going to take you back and see what you and Bower have to say. He may know something about this."

"If he does I don't believe he'll tell," said Jackson.

"Why not?" asked Tom, quickly.

"Because he's gone."

"Gone! Bower gone?"

"Yes," answered Jackson. "I saw him running out of the experiment shop as we raced along to help you. I didn't think, at the time, that he was doing more than go for aid, perhaps. But I see the game now."

"Oh, you mean—him?" and Tom pointed to the dripping figure.

"Yes," said Jackson in a low voice, as Koku went on ahead with his prisoner. "If, as you say, this man was in league with Bower, the latter has smelled a rat and skipped. He has run away, and I only hope he hasn't done any damage or got hold of any of your plans."

"We'll soon know about that," said Tom. "I wonder who is at the bottom of this?"

"Maybe those men you wouldn't work for," suggested the machinist.

"You mean Gale and Ware of the Universal Flying Machine Company?"

"Yes."

"Oh, I don't believe they'd stoop to any such measures as this—sending spies around," replied Tom. "But I can't be too careful. We'll investigate."

The first result of the investigation was to disclose the fact that Bower was gone. He had taken his few possessions and left the Swift plant while Tom was racing after the stranger. A hasty examination of the safe did not reveal anything missing, as Tom's plans and papers were intact. But they showed evidences of having been looked over, for they were out of the regular order in which the young inventor kept them.

"I begin to see it," said Tom, musingly. "Bower must have managed to open the safe while I was gone, and he must have made a hasty copy of some of the drawings of the silent motor, and passed them out of the window to this gold-tooth man, who tried to make off with them. Did you find anything on him?" he asked, as one of the men who had been instructed to search the stranger came into the office just then.

"Not a thing, Mr. Swift! Not a thing!" was the answer. "We took off every bit of his clothes and wrapped him in a blanket. He's in the engine room getting dry now. But there isn't a thing in any of his pockets."

"But I saw him stuffing some papers in as he ran away from me," said Tom. "We must be sure about this. And don't let the fellow get away until I question him."

"Oh, he's safe enough," answered the man. "Koku is guarding him. He won't get away."

"Then I'll have a look at his clothes," decided Tom. "He may have a secret pocket."

But nothing like this was disclosed, and the most careful search did not reveal anything incriminating in the man's garments.

"He might have thrown away any papers Bower gave him," said Tom. "Maybe they're at the bottom of the mud hole! If they're there they're safe enough. But have a search made of the ground where this man ran."

This was done, but without result. Some of the workmen

even dragged the mud hole without finding anything. Then Tom and his father had a talk with the stranger, who refused to give his name. The man was sullen and angry. He talked loudly about his innocence and of "having the law on" Tom for having tripped him into the mud.

"All right, if you want to make a complaint, go ahead," said the young inventor. "I'll make one against you for trespass. Why did you come on my grounds?"

"I was going to ask for work. I'm a good machinist and I wanted a job."

"How did you get in? Who admitted you at the gate?"

"I—I jest walked in," said the man, but Tom knew this could not be true, as no strangers were admitted without a permit and none had been issued. The man denied knowing anything about Bower, but the latter's flight was evidence enough that something was wrong.

Not wishing to go to the trouble of having the man arrested merely as a trespasser, Tom let him go after his clothes had been dried on a boiler in one of the shops.

"Take him to the gate, and tell him if he comes back he'll get another dose of the same kind of medicine," ordered Tom to one of the guards at the plant, and when the latter had reported that this had been done, he added in an earnest tone:

"He went off talking to himself and saying he'd get even with you, Mr. Swift."

"All right," said Tom easily. "I'll be on the watch."

The young inventor made a thorough examination of his experiment shop and the test motor. No damage seemed to have been done, and Tom began to think he had been too quick for the conspirators, if such they were. His plans and drawings were intact, and though Bower might have given a copy to the stranger with the gold tooth, the latter did not take any away with him. That he had some papers he wished to conceal and escape with, seemed certain, but the splash into the mud hole had ended this.

No trace was found of Bower, and an effort Tom made to ascertain if the man was a spy in the employ of Gale and Ware came to naught. The machinist had come well recommended, and the firm where he was last employed had nothing but good to say of him.

"Well, it's a mystery," decided Tom. "However, I got out of it pretty well. Only if that gold-tooth individual shows up again he won't get off so easily."

CHAPTER XI

A NIGHT TRIP

Taking a lesson from what had happened, Tom was very much more careful in the following experiments on his new, silent motor. He made some changes in his shop, and took Jackson in to help on the new machine, thus insuring perfect secrecy as the apparatus developed.

Tom also changed the safe in which he kept his plans, for the one he had used previous to the episode in which Bower and the stranger who took the mud bath figured, was one the combination of which could easily be ascertained by an expert. The new safe was more complicated, and Tom felt that his plans, specifications, and formulae which he had worked out were in less danger.

"I can just about figure out what happened," said Ned Newton to Tom, when told of the circumstances. "These Universal people were provoked because you wouldn't give them the benefit of your experience on their flying machines, and so they sent a spy to get work with you. They, perhaps, hoped to secure some of your ideas for their own, or they may have had a deeper motive."

"What deeper motive could they have, Ned?"

"They might have hoped to disable you, or some of your machines, so that you couldn't compete with them. They're unscrupulous, I hear, and will do anything to succeed and make money. So be on your guard against them."

"I will," Tom promised. "But I don't believe there's any more danger now. Anyhow, I have to take some chances."

"Yes, but be as careful as you can. How is the silent motor coming on?"

"Pretty good. I've had a lot of failures, and the thing isn't so easy as I at first imagined it would be. Noise is a funny thing, and I'm just beginning to understand some of the laws of acoustics we learned at high school. But I think I'm on the right track with the muffler and the cutting down of the noise of the explosions in the cylinders. I'm working both ends, you see—making a motor that doesn't cause as much racket as those now in use, and also providing means to take care of the noise that is made. It isn't possible to make a completely silent motor of an explosive gas type. The only thing that can be done is to kill the noise after it is made."

"What about the propeller blades?"

"Oh, they aren't giving me any trouble. The noise they make can't be heard a hundred feet in the air, but I am also working on improvements to the blades. Take it altogether, I'll have an almost silent aeroplane if my plans come out all right."

"Have you said anything to the government yet?"

"No; I want to have it pretty well perfected before I do. Besides, I don't want any publicity about it until I'm ready. If these Universal people are after me I'll fool 'em."

"That's right, Tom! Well, I must go. Another week of this Liberty Bond campaign!"

"I suppose you'll be glad when it's over."

"Well, I don't know," said Ned slowly. "It's part of my small contribution to Uncle Sam. I'm not like you—I can't invent things."

"But you have an awful smooth line of talk, Ned!" laughed

his chum. "I believe you could sell chloride of sodium to some of the fishes in the Great Salt Lake—that is if it has fishes."

"I don't know that it has, Tom. And, anyhow, I'm not posing as a salt salesman," and Ned grinned. "But I must really go. Our bank hasn't reached its quota in the sale of Liberty Bonds yet, and it's up to me to see that it doesn't fall down."

"Go to it, Ned! And I'll get busy on my silent motor."

"Getting busy" was Tom Swift's favorite occupation, and when he was working on a new idea, as was the case now, he was seldom idle, night or day.

"I have hardly seen you for two weeks," Mary Nestor wrote him one day. "Aren't you ever coming to see me any more, or take me for a ride?"

"Yes," Tom wrote back. "I'll be over soon. And perhaps on the next ride we take I won't have to shout at you through a speaking tube because the motor makes so much noise."

From this it may be gathered that Tom was on the verge of success. While not altogether satisfied with his progress, the young inventor felt that he was on the right track. There were certain changes that needed to be made in the apparatus he was building—certain refinements that must be added, and when this should be done Tom was pretty certain that he would have what would prove to be a very quiet aeroplane, if not an absolutely silent one.

The young inventor was engaged one day with some of the last details of the experiment. The new motor, with the silencer and the changed cylinders, had been attached to one of Tom's speedy aeroplanes, and he was making some intricate calculations in relation to a new cylinder block, to be used when he started to make a completely new machine of the improved type.

Tom had set down on paper some computations regarding

the cross-section of one of the cylinders, and was working out the amount of stress to which he could subject a shoulder strut, when a shadow was cast across the drawing board he had propped up in his lap.

In an instant Tom pulled a blank sheet over his mass of figures and looked up, a sudden fear coming over him that another spy was at hand. But a hearty voice reassured him.

"Bless my rice pudding!" cried Mr. Damon, "you shut yourself up here, Tom, like a hermit in the mountains. Why don't you come out and enjoy life?"

"Hello! Glad to see you!" cried Tom, joyfully. "You're just in time!"

"Time for what—dinner?" asked the eccentric man, with a chuckle. "If so, my reference to rice pudding was very proper."

"Why, yes, I imagine there must be a dinner in prospect somewhere, Mr. Damon," said Tom with a smile. "We'll have to see Mrs. Baggert about that. But what I meant was that you're just in time to have a ride with me, if you want to go."

"Go where?"

"Oh, up in cloudland. I have just finished my first sample of a silent motor, and I'm going to try it this evening. Would you like to come along?"

"I would!" exclaimed Mr. Damon. "Bless my onion soup, Tom, but I would! But why fly at night? Isn't it safer by daylight?"

"Oh, that doesn't make much difference. It's safe enough at any time. The reason I'm going to make my first flight after dark is that I don't want any spies about."

"Oh, I see! Are they camping on your trail?"

"Not exactly. But I can't tell where they may be. If I should start out in daylight and be forced to make a landing— Well, you know what a crowd always collects to see a stranded airship."

"That's right, Tom."

"That decided me to start off after dark. Then if we have to come down because of some sort of engine trouble or because my new attachment doesn't work right, we sha'n't have any prying eyes."

"I see! Well, Tom, I'll go with you. Fortunately I didn't tell my wife where I was going when I started out this afternoon, so she won't worry until after it's over, and then it won't hurt her. I'm ready any time you are."

"Good! Stay to dinner and I'll show you what I've made. Then we'll take a flight after dark."

This suited the eccentric man, and a little later, after he had eaten one of Mrs. Baggert's best meals, including rice pudding, of which he was very fond, Mr. Damon accompanied Tom to one of the big hangars where the new aeroplane had been set up.

"So that's the Air Scout, is it, Tom?" asked Mr. Damon, as he viewed the machine.

"Yes, that's the girl. 'Air Scout' is as good a name as any, until I see what she'll do."

"It doesn't look different from one of your regular craft of the skies, Tom."

"No, she isn't. The main difference is here," and Tom showed his friend where a peculiar apparatus had been attached to the motor. This was the silencer—the whole secret of the invention, so to speak.

To Mr. Damon it seemed to consist of an amazing collection of pipes, valves, baffle-plates, chambers, cylinders and reducers, which took the hot exhaust gases as they came from the motor and "ate them up," as he expressed it.

"The cylinders, too, and the spark plugs are differently arranged in the motor itself, if you could see them," said Tom to his friend. "But the main work of cutting down the noise is done right here," and he put his hand on the steel case attached to the motor, the case containing the apparatus already briefly described.

"Well, I'm ready when you are, Tom," said Mr. Damon.

"We'll go as soon as it's dark," was the reply. "But first I'll give you a demonstration. Start the motor, Jackson!" Tom called to his chief helper.

Mr. Damon had ridden in aeroplanes before, and had stood near when Tom started them; so he was prepared for a great rush of air as the propellers whirled about, and for deafening explosions from the engine.

The big blades, of new construction, were turned until the gas in the cylinders was sufficiently compressed. Then Jackson stepped back out of danger while Tom threw over the switch.

"Contact!" cried the young inventor.

Jackson gave the blades a quarter pull, and, a moment later, as he leaped back out of the way, they began to revolve with the swiftness of light. There was the familiar rush of air as the wooden wings cut through the atmosphere, but there was scarcely any noise. Mr. Damon could hardly believe his ears.

"I'm not running her at full speed," said Tom. "If I did she'd tear loose from the holding blocks. But you can see what little racket she makes."

"Bless my fountain pen!" cried Mr. Damon. "You are right, Tom Swift! Why, I can hear you talk almost as easily as if no engine were going. And I don't have to shout my head off, either."

This was perfectly true. Tom could converse with Mr. Damon in almost ordinary tones. The exhaust from the motor was nearly completely muffled.

"Out in the air it will seem even more quiet," said Tom. "I'll soon give you a chance to verify that statement."

He ran the engine a little longer, the aeroplane quivering with the vibrations, but remaining almost silent.

"I'm anxious to see what she'll do when in motion," said Tom, as he shut off the gas and spark.

Soon after supper, when the shades of evening were falling, he and Mr. Damon took their places in the first of the Air Scouts, to give it the preliminary test in actual flying.

Would Tom's hopes be justified or would he be disappointed?

CHAPTER XII

THE CRY FOR HELP

"All ready, Mr. Damon?" asked Tom, as he looked to see that all the levers, wheels, valves, and other controls were in working order on his Air Scout.

"As ready as I ever shall be, Tom," was the answer. "I don't know why it is, but somehow I feel that something is going to happen on this trip."

"Nonsense!" laughed Tom. "You're nervous; that's all."

"I suppose so. Don't think I'm going to back out, or anything like that, but I wish it were successfully over with, Tom Swift, I most certainly do."

"It will be in a little while," returned Tom, as he settled himself comfortably in his seat and pulled the safety strap tight. "You've gone up in this same plane before, when it didn't have the silent motor aboard."

"Yes, I know I have. Oh, I dare say it will be all right, Tom. And yet, somehow, I can't help feeling—"

But Tom Swift felt that the best way to set Mr. Damon's premonitions to rest was to start the motor, and this he gave orders to have done, Jackson and some others of the men from the shops congregating about the craft to see the beginning of the night flight. Mr. Swift was there also, and Eradicate. Mary Nestor had been invited, but her Red Cross work engaged her that evening, she said. Ned Newton was away from town on Liberty Bond business, and he could not be present at the test.

However, as Tom expected to have other trials when his motor was in even better shape, he was not exactly sorry for the absence of his friends.

"Contact!" called the young inventor, when Jackson had stepped back, indicating it was time to throw over the switch.

"Let her go!" cried Tom, and the next moment the motor was in operation, but so silently that his voice and that of Mr. Damon's could easily be heard above the machinery.

"Good, Tom! That's good!" cried Mr. Swift, and Tom easily heard his father's voice, though under other, and ordinary, circumstances this would have been impossible.

True, the hearing of Tom and Mr. Damon was muffled to a certain extent by the heavy leather and fur-lined caps they wore. But Tom had several small eyelet holes set into the flaps just over the opening of the ears, and these holes were sufficient to admit sounds, while keeping out most of the cold that obtains in the upper regions.

The aeroplane moved swiftly along the level starting ground, and away from the lighted hangars. Faster and faster it swung along as Tom headed it into the wind, and then, as the speed of the motor increased, the Air Scout suddenly left the earth and went soaring aloft as she had done before.

But there was this difference. She moved almost as silently as a great owl which swoops down out of the darkness—a bit of the velvety blackness itself. Up and up, and onward and onward, went the Air Scout. Tom Swift's improved, silent motor urged it onward, and as the young inventor listened to catch the noise of the machinery, his heart gave a bound of hope. For he could detect only very slight sounds.

"She's a success!" exulted Tom to himself. "She's a success, but she isn't perfect yet," he added. "I've got to make the muffler bigger and put in more baffle-plates. Then I think I can turn the trick."

He swung the machine out over the open country, and then, when they were up at a height and sailing along easily, he called back to Mr. Damon in the seat behind him:

"How do you like it?"

"Great!" exclaimed the eccentric man. "Bless my postage stamp, but it's great! Why, there's hardly a sound, Tom, and I can hear you quite easily."

"And I can hear you," added Tom. "I don't believe, down below there," and he nodded toward the earth, though Mr. Damon could not see this, as the airship, save for a tiny light over the instrument board, was in darkness, "they know that we're flying over their heads."

"I agree with you," was the answer. "Tom, my boy, I believe you've solved the trick! You have produced a silent aeroplane, and now it's up to the government to make use of it."

"I'm not quite ready for that yet," replied the young inventor. "I have several improvements to make. But, when they are finished, I'll let Uncle Sam know what I have. Then it's up to him."

"And you must be careful, Tom, that some of your rivals don't hear of your success and get it away from you," warned Mr. Damon, as Tom guided the Air Scout along the aerial way—an unlighted and limitless path in the silent darkness.

"Oh, they'll have to get up pretty early in the morning to do that!" boasted Tom, and afterward he was to recall those words with a bit of chagrin.

On and on they sailed, and as Tom increased the speed of the motor, and noted how silently it ran, he began to have high hopes that he had builded better than he knew. For even with the motor running at almost full speed there was not noise enough to hinder talk between himself and Mr. Damon.

Of course there was some little sound. Even the most perfect electric motor has a sort of hum which can be detected when one is close to it. But at a little distance a great dynamo in operation appears to be silence itself.

"I can go this one better, though," said Tom as he sailed along in the night. "I see where I've made a few mistakes in the baffle plate of the silencer. I'll correct that and—"

As he spoke the machine gave a lurch, and the motor, instead of remaining silent, began to cough and splutter as in the former days.

"Bless my rubber boots, Tom! what's the matter?" cried Mr. Damon.

"Something's gone wrong," Tom answered, barely able to hear and make himself heard above the sudden noise. "I'll have to shut off the power and glide down. We can make a landing in this big field," for just then the moon came out from behind a cloud, and Tom saw, below them, a great meadow, not far from the home of Mary Nestor. He had often landed in this same place.

"Something has broken in the muffler, I think, letting out some of the exhaust," he said to Mr. Damon, for, now that the motor was shut off, Tom could speak in his ordinary tones. "I'll soon have it fixed, or, if I can't, we can go back in the old style —with the machine making as much racket as it pleases."

So Tom guided the machine down. It went silently now, of course, making, with the motor shut off, no more sound than a falling leaf. Down to the soft, springy turf in the green meadow Tom guided the machine. As it came to a stop, and he and Mr. Damon got out, there was borne to their ears a wild cry:

"Help! Help!"

CHAPTER XIII

SOMETHING QUEER

"Did you hear that?" asked Tom Swift of his companion.

"Hear it? Bless my ear drums, I should say I did hear it! Some one is in trouble, Tom. Caught in a bog, most likely, the same as that spy chap who was at your place. That's it—caught in a bog!"

"There isn't any bog or swamp around here, Mr. Damon. If there was I shouldn't have tried a landing. No, it's something else besides that. Hark!"

Again the cry sounded, seeming to come from a point behind the landing place of the silent airship. It was clear and distinct:

"Help! Help! They are—"

The voice seemed to die away in a gurgle, as though the person's mouth had been covered quickly.

"He's sinking, Tom! He's sinking!" cried Mr. Damon. "I once heard a man who almost drowned cry out, and it sounded exactly like that!"

"But there isn't any water around here for any one to drown in," declared Tom. "It's a big, dry meadow. I know where we are."

"Then what is it?"

"I don't know, but we're going to find out. Some one attacked by some one else—or something, I should say," ventured the young inventor.

"Something! do you mean a wild beast, Tom?"

"No, for there aren't any of those here any more than there is water. Though it may be that some farmer's bull or a savage dog has got loose and has attacked some traveler. But, in that case I think we would hear bellows or barks, and all I heard was a cry for help."

"The same with me, Tom. Let's investigate;"

"That's what I intend doing. Come on. The airship will be all right until we come back."

"Better take a light—hadn't you? It's dark, even if the moon does show now and then," suggested Mr. Damon.

"Guess you are right," agreed Tom. Aboard his airship there were several small but powerful portable electric lights, and after securing one of these Tom and Mr. Damon started for the spot whence the call for help had come. As they walked along, their feet making no noise on the soft turf, they listened intently for a repetition of the call for aid.

"I don't hear anything," said Tom, after a bit.

"Nor I," added Mr. Damon. "We don't know exactly which way to go, Tom."

"That's right. Guess we'd better give him a hail; whoever it is."

Tom came to a halt, and raising his voice to a shout called:

"Hello there! What's the matter? We'll help you if you can tell us which way to come!"

They both listened intently, but no voice answered them. At the same time, however, they were aware of a sound as of hurrying feet, and there seemed to be muttered imprecations not far away. Tom and Mr. Damon looked in the direction of the sound, and the young inventor flashed his light. But there was a clump of bushes and trees at that point and the electrical rays did not penetrate very far.

"Some one's over there!" exclaimed Tom in a whisper. "We'd better go and see what it is."

"All right," agreed Mr. Damon, and he, too, spoke in a low voice.

Why they did this when their previous talk had been in ordinary tones, and when Tom had shouted so loudly, they did not stop to reason about or explain just then. But later they both admitted that they whispered because they thought there was something wrong on foot—because they feared a crime was being committed and they wanted to surprise the perpetrators if they could.

And it was this fact of their whispering that enabled the two to hear something that, otherwise, they might not have heard. And this was the sound of some vehicle hurrying away—an automobile, if Tom was any judge. The cries for help had been succeeded by stifled vocal sounds, and these, in turn, by the noise of wheels on the ground.

"What does it all mean?" asked Mr. Damon in a whisper.

"I don't know," answered Tom, resolutely, "but we've got to find out. Come on."

They advanced toward the dark clump of trees and low bushes. There was no need to be especially cautious in regard to being silent, as their feet made little, if any, sound on the deep grass. And, as Tom walked in advance, now and then flashing his light, Mr. Damon suddenly caught him by the coat.

"What is it?" asked the young inventor.

"Look! Just over the top of that hill, where the moon shines. Don't you see an automobile outlined?"

Tom looked quickly.

"I do," he answered. "There's a road from here, just the other side of those trees, to that hill. The auto must have gone that way. Well, there's no use in trying to follow it now. Whoever it was has gotten away."

"But they may have left some one behind, Tom. We'd better look in and around those trees."

"I suppose we had, but I don't believe we'll find anything. I can pretty nearly guess, now, what it was."

"What?" asked Mr. Damon.

"Well, some chauffeur was out for a ride in his employer's car without permission. He got here, had an accident—maybe some friends he took for a ride were hurt and they called for help. The chauffeur knew if there was any publicity he'd be blamed, and so he got away as quickly as he could. Guess the accident—if that's what it was—didn't amount to much, or they couldn't have run the car off. We've had our trouble for our pains."

"Well, maybe you're right, Tom Swift, but all the same, I'd like to have a look among those trees," said Mr. Damon.

"Oh. we'll look, all right," assented Tom, "but I doubt if we find anything."

And he was right. They walked in and about the little grove, flashing the light at intervals, but beyond marks of auto wheels in the dust of the road, which was near the clump of maples, there was nothing to indicate what had happened.

"Though there was some sort of fracas," declared Tom. "Look where the dust is trampled down. There were several men here, perhaps skylarking, or perhaps it was a fight."

"Some one must have been hurt, or they wouldn't have cried for help," said Mr. Damon.

"Well, that's so. But perhaps it was some one not used to riding in autos, and he may have imagined the accident was worse than it was, and called for help involuntarily. There is no evidence of any serious accident having happened—no spots of blood, at any rate," and Tom laughed at his own grimness. "It was a new car, too, or at least one with new tires on."

"How do you know?" asked Mr. Damon.

"Tell by the plain marks of the rubber tread in the dust," was the answer. "Look," and Tom pointed to the wheel marks in the focus of his electric lamp. "It's a new tire, too, with square protuberances on the tread instead of the usual diamond or round ones. A new kind of tire, all right."

He and Mr. Damon remained for a few minutes looking about the place whence had come the calls for help, and then the eccentric man remarked:

"Well, as long as we can't do anything here, Tom, we might as well travel on; what do you say?"

"I agree with you. There isn't any use in staying. We'll get the Air Scout fixed up and travel back home. But this was something queer," mused Tom. "I hope it doesn't turn out later that a crime has been committed, and we didn't show enough gumption to prevent it."

"We couldn't prevent it. We heard the cries as soon as we landed."

"Yes, but if we had rushed over at once we might have caught the fellows. But I guess it was only a slight accident, and some one was more frightened than hurt. We'll have to let it go at that."

But the more he thought about it the more Tom Swift thought there was something queer in that weird cry for help on the lonely meadow in the darkness of the night.

CHAPTER XIV

THE TELEPHONE CALL

The defect in the motor which had caused Tom Swift to shut off the power and drift down to earth was soon remedied, once the young inventor began an examination of the craft. One of the oil feeds had become choked and this automatically cut down the gasoline supply, causing one or more cylinders to miss. It was a safety device Tom had installed to prevent the motor running dry, and so being damaged.

Once the clogged oil feed was cleared the motor ran as before, and just as silently, though, as Tom had said, he was not entirely satisfied with the quietness, but intended to do further work toward perfecting it.

"I'll start the propellers now, Mr. Damon," said Tom, when the trouble had been remedied. "You know how to throw the switch, don't you?"

"I guess so," was the answer. Mr. Damon and Tom had traveled so often together in gasoline craft that the young inventor had taught his friend certain fundamentals about them, and in an emergency the eccentric man could help start an aeroplane. This he now did, taking charge of the controls which could be operated from his seat as well as from Tom's. Tom whirled the propellers, and soon the motor was in motion.

Mr. Damon, once the big wooden blades were revolving, slowed down the apparatus until Tom could jump aboard, after which the latter took charge and soon speeded up the machine, sending it aloft.

As the green meadow, dimly seen in the light of the moon, seemed to drop away below them, and the clump of trees vanished from sight, both Tom and Mr. Damon wondered who it was that had called for help, and if the matter were at all serious. They were inclined to think it was not, but Tom could not rid himself of a faint suspicion that there might have been trouble.

However, thoughts of his new silent Air Scout soon drove everything else from his mind, and as he guided the comparatively silent machine on its quiet way toward his own home he was thinking how he could best improve the muffler.

"Well, here we are again, safe and sound," remarked Tom, as he brought the craft to a stop in front of the hangar, and Jackson and his helpers, who were awaiting the return, hurried out to take charge.

"Yes, everything seems to point to success, Tom," agreed Mr. Damon. "That is, unless the slight accident we had means trouble."

"Oh, no, that had nothing to do with the operation of the silencer. But I'm going to do better yet. Some day I'll take you for a ride in a silent machine which will make so little noise that you can hear a pin drop."

"Well," remarked Mr. Damon' with a laugh, "I don't know that listening to falling pins will give me any great amount of pleasure, Tom, but I appreciate your meaning."

"Everything all right?" asked Mr. Swift, as he came out to hear the details from his son. "Do you think you have solved the problem?"

"Not completely, but I'll soon be able to write Q. E. D. after it. Some refinements are all that are needed, Dad."

"Glad to hear it. I was a bit anxious."

Mr. Swift questioned his son about the technical details of

the trip, asking how the motor had acted under the pressure caused by so completely muffling the exhaust, and for some minutes the two inventors, young and old, indulged in talk which was not at all interesting to Mr. Damon. They went into the house, and Tom asked to have a little lunch, which Mrs. Baggert set out for him.

"It's rather late to eat," said the young inventor, "but I always feel hungry after I test a new machine and find that it works pretty well. Will you join me in a sandwich or two, Mr. Damon?"

"Why, bless my ketchup bottle, I believe I will."

And so they ate and talked. Tom was on the point of telling his father something of the queer cry for help they had heard on the lonely meadow when Mrs. Baggert produced a letter which she said had come for Tom that afternoon, but had been mislaid by a new maid who had been engaged to help with the housework.

"She took it to the shop after you had left, and only now told me about it," explained Mrs. Baggert. "So I sent Eradicate for it."

"How long ago was that?" asked Tom, as he took the missive.

"Oh, an hour ago," answered Mrs. Baggert, with a smile. "But don't blame poor Rad for that. He wanted to deliver the letter to you personally, and so did Koku. The result was your giant kept after Rad, trying to get the letter from him, and Rad kept hiding and slinking about for a chance to see you himself until I saw what was going on, a little while ago, and took the letter myself. Else you might never have gotten it, so jealous are those two," and Mrs. Baggert laughed.

"Guess it isn't of much importance," Tom said, as he tore open the envelope. "It's from the Universal Flying Machine

Company, of New York, and I imagine they're trying to get me to reconsider my refusal to link up with them."

"Yes," he went on, as he read the missive, "that's it. They've raised the amount to thirty thousand a year now, Dad, and they say they feel sure I shall regret it if I do not accept.

"This is a bit queer, though," went on the young inventor. "This letter was written three days ago, but it reached Shopton only to-day. And it says that unless they hear from me at once they will have to take steps that will cause me great inconvenience. They have nerve, at any rate, and impudence, too! I won't even bother to answer. But I wonder what they mean, and why this letter was delayed?"

"The mails are all late on account of the transportation congestion caused by moving troops to the camps," said Mr. Damon. "Some of my letters are delayed a week. But, as you say, Tom, these fellows are very impudent to threaten that way."

"It's all bluff," declared Tom. "I'm not worrying. And now, Dad, since I've almost reached the top of the hill with my Air Scout, I may be able to help you on that new electric motor you're puzzling over."

"I wish you would, Tom. I am trying to invent a new system of interchangeable brush contacts, but so far I've been unable to make them work. However, there is no great hurry about that. If you are going to offer your silent machine to the government finish that first. We need all the aircraft we can get. The battles on the other side seem to be all in favor of the Germans, so far."

"We haven't got into our stride yet," declared Mr. Damon. "Once Uncle Sam gets the boys over there in force, there'll be a different story to tell. I only wish—"

At that moment the telephone set up an insistent ringing, breaking in on Mr. Damon's remarks.

"I'll answer," said Tom, as Mrs. Baggert moved toward the instrument, which was an extension from the main one.

"Hello!" called the young inventor into the transmitter, and as he received an answer a look of pleasure came over his face.

"Yes, Mary, this is Tom," he said. He remained silent a moment, while it was evident he was listening to the voice at the other end of the wire. Then he suddenly exclaimed:

"What's that? Tell him to come home? Why, he isn't here. I just came in and—what—wait a minute!"

With a rather strange look on his face Tom covered the mouth-piece of the instrument with his hand, and, turning to his father, asked:

"Is Mr. Nestor here?"

"No," replied Mr. Swift slowly, "He was here, though. He came a little while after you and Mr. Damon started off in the Air Scout. But he didn't stay. Said he wanted to see you about something and would call again."

"Oh," remarked the young man. "I didn't know he had been there."

"I meant to tell you," said Mrs. Baggert; "but getting the lunch made me forget it, I guess."

Tom uncovered the transmitter of the telephone again, and spoke to Mary Nestor.

"Hello," he said. "I was wrong, Mary. Your father was here, but he left when he found I wasn't at home. How long ago? Wait a minute and I'll inquire.

"How long ago did Mr. Nestor leave?" asked the young inventor of the housekeeper. "Nearly an hour," he said into the instrument, after he had received the answer. Then, after listening a moment, he added: "Yes, I guess he'll be home soon now. Probably stopped down town to see some of his friends. Yes, Mr. Damon and I tried out the Air Scout. Yes, she worked pretty well, for a starter, but there is something yet to be done. Oh, yes, now I'll have time to come over to see you, and take you for a ride too. We won't have to talk through a speaking tube, either. Tell your father I am sorry I was out when he called. I'll come to see him to-morrow, if he wants me to. Yes—yes. I guess so!" and Tom laughed, it being evident that his remarks at the end of the conversation had to do with personal matters.

"A telegram has come for Mr. Nestor and they were anxious that he should get it," Tom explained to his little audience as he hung up the receiver and put aside the telephone. "I wonder what he wanted to see me about?"

"He didn't say," replied Mrs. Baggert.

Mr. Damon, Tom, and his father remained in conversation a little while longer, and the eccentric man was thinking that it was about time for him to return home, when the telephone rang again.

"Hello," answered Tom, as he was nearest the instrument. "Oh, yes, Mary, this is he. What's that? Your father hasn't reached home yet? And your mother is worried? Oh tell her there is no cause for alarm. As I said, he probably stopped on his way to see some friends."

Tom listened for perhaps half a minute to a talk that was inaudible to the others in the room, and they noticed a grave look come over his face. Then he said:

"I'll be right over, Mary. Yes, I'll come at once. And tell your mother not to worry. I'm sure nothing could have happened. I'll be with you in a jiffy!"

As Tom Swift hung up the receiver he said:

"Mr. Nestor hasn't reached home yet, and as he promised to return at once in case he didn't find me, his wife is much worried. I'll go over and see what I can do."

"I'll come along!" volunteered Mr. Damon. "It isn't late yet."

"Yes, do come," urged Tom. "But I suppose when we get there we'll find our friend has arrived safely. We'll go over in the electric runabout."

CHAPTER XV

A VAIN SEARCH

Tom Swift's speedy little electric car was soon at the door in readiness to take him and Mr. Damon to the Nestor home. The electric runabout was a machine Tom had evolved in his early inventive days, and though he had other automobiles, none was quite so fast or so simple to run as this, which well merited the name of the most rapid machine on the road. In it Tom had once won a great race, as has been related in the book bearing the title, "Tom Swift and His Electric Runabout."

"Mary didn't telephone again, did she?" Tom asked his father, as he stopped at the house to get Mr. Damon, having gone out to see about getting the electric runabout in readiness.

"No," was the answer. "The telephone hasn't rung since."

"Then, I guess, Mr. Nestor can't have arrived home," said Tom. "It's a bit queer, his delay, but I'm sure it will be explained naturally. Only Mary and her mother are alone and, very likely, they're nervous. I'll telephone to let you know everything is all right as soon as I get there," Tom promised his father and Mrs. Baggert as he drove off down the road, partly illuminated by the new moon.

Rapidly and almost as silently as his Air Scout Tom Swift drove the speedy car down the highway. It was about three miles from his home to that of Mary Nestor, and though the distance was quickly covered, to Tom, at least, the space seemed interminable. But at length he drove up to the door. There were lights in most of the rooms, which was unusual at this time of night.

The sound of the wheels had not ceased echoing on the gravel of the drive before Mary was out on the porch, which she illuminated by an overhead light.

"Oh, Tom," she cried, "he hasn't come yet, and we are so worried! Did you see anything of father as you came along?"

"No," was Tom's answer. "But we didn't look for him along the road, as we came by the turnpike, and he wouldn't travel that way. But he will be along at any moment now. You must remember it's quite a walk from my house, and—"

"But he was on his bicycle," said Mary. "We wanted him to go in the auto, but he said he wanted some exercise after supper, and he went over on his wheel. He said he'd be right back, but he hasn't come yet."

"Oh, he will!" said Tom reassuringly. "He may have had a puncture, or something like that. Bicyclists are just as liable to them as autoists," he added with a laugh.

"Well, I'm sure I hope it will be all right," sighed Mary. "I wish you could convince mother to that effect. She's as nervous as a cat. Come in and tell us what to do."

"Oh, he'll be all right," declared Mr. Damon, adding his assurances to Tom's.

They found Mrs. Nestor verging on an attack of hysteria. Though Mr. Nestor often went out during the evening, he seldom stayed late.

"And he said he'd be right back if he found you weren't at home, Tom," said Mrs. Nestor. "I'm sure I don't know what can be keeping him!"

"It's too soon to get worried yet," replied the young inventor cheerfully. "I'll wait a little while, and then, if he doesn't come, Mr. Damon and I will go back over the road and look carefully.

He may have had a slight fall—sprained his ankle or something like that—and not be able to ride. We came by the turnpike, a road he probably wouldn't take on his wheel. He's all right, you may be sure of that."

Tom tried to speak reassuringly, but somehow, he did not believe himself. He was beginning to think more and more how strange it was that Mr. Nestor did not return home.

"We'll wait just a bit longer before setting out on a search," he told Mary and her mother. "But I'm sure he will be along any minute now."

They went into the library, Mary and her mother, Tom and Mr. Damon. And there they sat waiting. Tom tried to entertain Mary and Mrs. Nestor with an account of his trial trip in the Air Scout, but the two women scarcely heard what he said.

All sat watching the clock, and looking from that to the telephone, which they tried to hope would ring momentarily and transmit to them good news. Then they would listen for the sound of footsteps or bicycle wheels on the gravel walk. But they heard nothing, and as the seconds were ticked off on the clock the nervousness of Mrs. Nestor increased, until she exclaimed:

"I can stand it no longer! We must notify the police—or do something!"

"I wouldn't notify the police just yet," counseled Tom. "Mr. Damon and I will start out and look along the road. If it should happen, as will probably turn out to be the case, that Mr. Nestor has met with only a simple accident, he would not like the notoriety, or publicity, of having the police notified."

"No, I am sure he would not," agreed Mary. "Tom's way is best, Mother."

"All right, just as you say, only find my husband," and Mrs. Nestor sighed, and turned her head away.

"Even if Mr. Nestor had had a fall," reasoned Tom, "he could call for help, and get some one to telephone, unless—"

And as he reasoned thus Tom Swift gave a mental start at his own use of the word "help."

That weird cry on the lonely meadow came back to him with startling distinctness.

"Come on, Mr. Damon!" cried Tom, in a voice he tried to make cheerful. "We'll find that Mr. Nestor is probably walking along, carrying his disabled bicycle instead of having it carry him. We'll soon have him safe back to you," he called to the two women.

"I wish I could go with you, and help search," observed Mary.

"Oh, I couldn't bear to be left alone!" exclaimed her mother.

"We'll telephone as soon as we find him," called Tom to Mrs. Nestor, as he and Mr. Damon again got into the runabout and started away from the place.

"What do you think of it, Tom?" asked the eccentric man, when they were once more on the road.

"Why, nothing much—as yet," Tom said. "That is, I think nothing more than a simple accident has happened, if, indeed, it is anything more than that he has delayed to talk to some friends."

"Would he delay this long?"

"I don't know."

"And then, Tom—bless my spectacles! what of that cry we heard? Could that have been Mr. Nestor?"

There! It was out! The suspicion that Tom had been trying to keep his mind away from came to the fore. Well, he might as well race the issue now as later.

"I've been thinking of that," he told Mr. Damon. "It might have been Mary's father calling for help."

"But we looked, Tom, near the trees, and couldn't discover anything. If he had been calling for help—"

Mr. Damon did not finish.

"He may have fallen from his wheel and been hurt," said Tom, as he turned the electric runabout into the highway that Mr. Nestor would, most likely, have taken on his way from Shopton. "Then he may have called for help, and some autoists, passing, may have heard and taken him away."

"Yes, but where, Tom? Whoever called for help was taken away, that's sure. But where?"

"To some hospital, I suppose."

"Then hadn't we better inquire there? There are only two hospitals of any account around here. The one in Shopton and the one in Waterfield. My wife is on the board of Lady Managers there. We could call that hospital up and—"

"We'll look along the road first," said Tom. "If we begin to make inquiries at the hospitals there will be a lot of questions asked, and a general alarm may be sent out. Mr. Nestor wouldn't like that, if he isn't in any danger. And it may turn out that he has met an old friend, and has been talking with him all this while, forgetting all about the passage of time."

They were now driving along the highway that led from the little suburb where Mr. Nestor lived, to the main part of Shopton, just beyond which was Tom's home. This section was country-like, with very few houses and those placed at rather infrequent intervals. The road was a good one, though not the main-traveled one, and Mr. Nestor, as was known, frequently used it when he rode his bicycle, an exercise of which he was very fond.

As Tom and Mr. Damon drove along, they scanned, as best they could in the light from the young moon and the powerful lamps on the runabout, every part of the highway. They were looking for some dark blot which might indicate where a man had fallen from his wheel and was lying in some huddled heap on the road. But they saw nothing like this, much to their relief.

"Do you know, Tom," said Mr. Damon, when they were nearing the town, and their search, thus far, had been in vain, "I think we're going at this the wrong way."

"Why, so?"

"Because Mr. Nestor may have fallen, and been hurt, and have been carried into any one of a dozen houses along the road. In that case we wouldn't see him. We've passed over the most lonely part of the journey and haven't seen him. If the accident occurred near the houses his cries would have brought some one out to help him. He is well known around here, and, even if he were unconscious and couldn't tell who he was, he could be identified by papers in his pockets. Then his family would be notified by telephone."

"Perhaps you are right, Mr. Damon. We may be wasting time this way. What do you suggest?" asked Tom.

"That we don't delay any longer, but call up the hospitals at once. If he isn't in either of those he must be in some house, and in such condition that his identity cannot be established. In that event it is a case for the police. We haven't found him, and I think we had better give the alarm."

Tom Swift thought it over for a moment. Then he came to a sudden decision.

"You're right!" he told Mr. Damon. "We mustn't waste any more time. He isn't along the road he ought to have traveled in coming from my house to his home—that's sure. But before I call up the hospitals I want to try out one more idea."

"What's that, Tom?"

"I want to go to the place where we heard that cry for help."

"Do you think that could have been Mr. Nestor?"

"It may have been. We'll go and take another look around there. Some man was evidently hurt there, and was taken away. We may get a clew. The lights on the runabout will give us a better chance to look around than we had by the little pocket lamp. We'll try there, and, if we don't find anything, then I'll call up the hospitals."

CHAPTER XVI

THE LONG NIGHT

With the speedy runabout it did not take Tom Swift and Mr. Damon long to reach the place where the Air Scout had been grounded a few hours before, and where they had heard the cry for help. All was as dark and as silent as when they had been there before.

But, as Tom had said, the lights from his electric runabout would give a brilliant illumination, and these he now directed toward the clump of trees whence the cry for help had seemed to come.

"Doesn't appear to have been visited by any one since we were here," remarked Tom, as he observed the marks of the new automobile tire in the dust. "Now we'll look about more carefully."

This they did, but they were about to give up in despair and start for the nearest telephone to call up the hospitals, when Mr. Damon gave an exclamation.

"What is it?" asked Tom.

"Something bright and shining!" said his companion. "I saw it gleam in the light of the lamps. You nearly put your foot on it, Tom. Just step back a moment."

Tom did so, and the eccentric man, with another exclamation, this time of satisfaction, reached down and picked something up from the dusty road.

"It's a watch!" he exclaimed. "A gold watch! And it's been stepped on, evidently, or run over by an auto. Not much damaged, but the case is a bit bent and scratched. It's stopped, too!" he added as he held it to his ear.

"What time does it show?" asked Tom.

"Eight forty-seven," answered Mr. Damon, as he consulted the dial. "Why, Tom, that was just about when we heard the cries for help!"

"Yes, it must have been. Let me see that watch."

No sooner had the young inventor taken the timepiece into his hands than he, too, uttered a cry of amazement.

"Do you recognize it?" asked Mr. Damon, in great excitement.

"It's Mr. Nestor's watch!" cried Tom. "He must have fallen here, and been hurt. It was Mr. Nestor who cried for help, and who was taken away by the autoists. They've probably taken him to some hospital. There's been an accident all right."

Tom and Mr. Damon were of one mind now in thinking that Mr. Nestor had met with some mishap on the road—an automobile accident most likely—and that he was the person who had called for help.

"If they had only answered when we hallooed at them," said Tom, "we wouldn't be in all this stew now. We could have told the strangers who came to his aid who he was, and we might even have taken him to the hospital in the airship."

"Well, it's too late to think of that now," returned Mr. Damon. "We had better get into communication with him as soon as we can, and then send word to his wife and daughter. I hope he isn't badly hurt."

Tom hoped so, too, with all his heart.

There was nothing to do but to get back in the runabout and make all speed for the nearest telephone, and Tom Swift lost little time in doing this. They found a drug store which was open a little later than usual, and at once Tom went into the booth and called up the Shopton hospital. He was well known there, as he and his father were liberal supporters of the institution, which was a private affair. Many of Tom's men were treated at the dispensary, and, as accidents were of more or less frequent occurrence at the works, the young inventor had frequent occasions to call up the place.

"Mr. Nestor would ask to be taken there, as it's nearest his home—that is, if he was able to speak," Tom said to Mr. Damon, who agreed with him. There was a little delay in getting the hospital on the wire, but when Tom had it, and was talking to the superintendent, he was rather surprised, to tell the truth, to be told that Mr. Nestor had not been brought in.

"We haven't had any accident cases all day, nor to-night, Mr. Swift," the superintendent reported. "Was this some one special you were inquiring about?"

For Tom, determining not to give Mr. Nestor's name, except as a last resort, had merely inquired whether any recent accident cases had been brought in.

"I'll let you know later, Mr. Millard," he told the superintendent, not exactly answering the question. He hung up the receiver, and, opening the door of the booth, said to Mr. Damon: "He isn't there."

"Then try Waterfield," was the suggestion; and Tom did so, though he could not imagine why an injured man, such as Mr. Nestor might prove to be, should be taken as far as Waterfield, when the hospital at Shopton was nearer.

"Unless," he told Mr. Damon, "the people which ran down Mary's father didn't know about our hospital."

The reply from the institution in Mr. Damon's home town was just as discouraging as had been the answer from Shopton. At first, when Tom inquired, the head nurse had said there was an accident case at that moment being brought in. Tom was all excitement until she went to inquire the name and circumstances, and then he learned that it was the case of a little boy who had fallen downstairs at his home and broken a leg. There was no record of any one answering the description of Mr. Nestor having been brought in that evening.

"Hum! This is getting to be mysterious," mused Tom, as he came out of the booth. "What shall we do—go back and tell Mrs. Nestor and Mary, or communicate with the police?"

"Why not try the Alexian Hospital?" asked Mr. Damon. "That's away over in Centerford, to be sure, but it's more likely to be known to passing tourists than either of our institutions around here, especially if the autoists were strangers."

"That's so," agreed Tom. The Alexian Hospital was operated under the direction of the Brothers of that faith, and was well known in that part of the state. Often cases of persons who had been injured by passing automobiles had been taken there for treatment, for, as Mr. Damon had said, it was well known, and Centerford was the nearest large city.

"I can just about see how it happened," said Tom. "They ran Mr. Nestor down, and stopped to pick him up after they heard his cries for help. And the Alexian Hospital was the first one they thought of. We should have called that up first."

But once more disappointment awaited the young inventor and his friend. Word came back over the wire that no accident case, which bore any resemblance to Mary's father, had been brought in.

"Well, I'm stumped!" exclaimed Tom. "What shall we do now, Mr. Damon?"

"Much as I dislike it," said the eccentric man who was too much worried, now, to do any "blessing," which was his favorite expression, "I think we ought to communicate with Mrs. Nestor. She will be very anxious."

"I guess we'll have to," said Tom. "But wait! I'll call up my house first, and see if he has gone back there."

But Mr. Nestor had not done this, and Mrs. Baggert, who answered the telephone, said Mary had been calling frantically for Tom, as her mother was now on the verge of complete collapse.

"No help for it," said Tom, ruefully. "We've got to tell 'em we have no news, and can't find him."

And, hearing this, Mrs. Nestor did collapse, and a doctor was called in.

Thereupon Tom, who with Mr. Damon had gone back to the Nestor home, took charge of matters, sending for Mrs. Nestor's sister to come and stay with her and take charge of the house.

"You'll need some one to stay with you," he told Mary.

"Yes, I shall," she admitted, trying bravely not to give way to her emotion. "Oh, Tom, I wish you could stay, too. I'm sure something dreadful must have happened to poor father. Please stay and help us find him!"

"I will," Tom promised. "As soon as your aunt comes I'll take Mr. Damon home, and then I'll give the rest of my time to you."

And this Tom did, sending word home that he would remain at the Nestor's all night and part of the next day.

Tom got but little sleep that night. He communicated with the police and saw to it that a general alarm was sent out. He called up all hospitals within a radius of fifty miles, but could get no trace of any injured man whose description resembled that of Mr. Nestor.

"What can have happened?" asked Mary tearfully.

"Well, the way I figure it out is this," said Tom. "Your father left my house soon after Mr. Damon and I did in the Air Scout.

Mr. Nestor was riding his bicycle, and he must have been run into by an automobile. That is how his watch was damaged and that was when Mr. Damon and I heard the cries for help."

"Oh, do you think he was badly hurt?" asked Mary.

"No, I don't," and Tom answered truthfully. "The voice sounded as though he was in pain, certainly, but it was strong and vigorous, and not at all as though he was dangerously hurt."

"And what do you think happened to him after he was hurt?" asked Mary.

"The autoists took him away," decided Tom. "In fact, we heard the machine go, but of course we never connected the call for help and what followed with your father. The autoists took him away."

"Where?"

"I should say to some hospital. Perhaps a private one of which we know nothing, and which may be near here. I'll get a full list from the Board of Health to-morrow. Or it may be that the autoists, seeing the damage they had done, took your father to the home of one of themselves, and summoned a doctor there."

"Why would they do that?"

"Well, they may have been so frightened they didn't realize what they were doing, or they may have thought he would get better treatment in a private house, if he were not badly injured, than if he should be taken to a hospital. It may have been that one of the persons in the auto was a physician, and wished to try his own skill on the man he had hurt."

"You make me feel more comfortable, Tom," said Mary. "But, even supposing all this, why couldn't they telephone to us that my father was all right? He always carries an identification card with him, and if he were unconscious it could be ascertained who he was."

"That's what I can't understand," said Tom frankly. "It puzzles me. But we'll find him—never fear!"

And so he kept on with his telephone inquiries, while a physician and her sister ministered to Mrs. Nestor. The night was very, very long, and no good news came in.

CHAPTER XVII

SILENT SAM

Slowly the dawn broke through the mists of darkness, and made the earth light. The sun came straggling in through cracks in the shutters in the home of Mr. Nestor, the gradually increasing gleam paling the electric lights, in the glare of which Tom Swift, Mary, and her aunt sat, waiting for some word of the missing man. But none came.

"What shall we do now?" asked Mary, as she looked at Tom.

"Oh, there's lots to do," he said, trying to make his voice sound cheerful. "We'll be busy all day. I sent word to have one of my touring cars ready to hurry to any part of the country the moment we should get word from your father."

"And do you think we shall get word, Tom?" the girl went on wistfully.

"Of course we shall!" he cried. "Word may come in at any time. Now get ready, eat a good breakfast, and then you can go with me as soon as we hear anything definite. Come, we'll have breakfast!"

"I can't eat a thing!" protested Mary.

"Oh, yes you can," said her aunt, who was a cheerful sort of person. "I'll see about getting something for you and Mr. Swift, and see that your mother is all right."

She left the room to give orders to the servant about the meal, and returned to say that Mrs. Nestor was sleeping quietly. She had been given a sedative. Mary managed to eat a little, and she gave Tom the address of several friends who were called up in the vain hope that, somehow, Mr. Nestor might have gone to see them.

"Tom, what do you really think has happened?" asked Mary again, as they sat facing one another in the library, during a respite from the telephone.

Tom Swift repeated, to the girl his theory of what had happened with an assumption of confidence he did not altogether feel.

His prediction of a speedy end to the suspense did not come true that day, nor for many days. No news was heard of Mr. Nestor. After the first day, when there was no information and when no reports came of any one of his description having been hurt in an automobile accident or having been taken to any hospital, the police started an energetic search.

The authorities in all near-by cities were notified, and all thought of keeping from the public what had happened was given over. Tom's story, of how he and Mr. Damon had heard the cry for help on the lonely meadow, was printed in the papers, though the young inventor did not say that he had been out trying his new aeroplane. That was a detail not needed in the finding of Mr. Nestor.

But Mary's father was not found. The mystery regarding his disappearance deepened, and there was no trace of him after he had left Tom's house that eventful evening. Persons living along the roads he might have taken in riding his bicycle were questioned, but they had seen nothing of him, nor were they aware of any accident. Tom's testimony and that of Mr. Damon was all the clew there was.

"I don't believe he's dead!" stoutly declared the young inventor, when this dire possibility had been hinted at. "I believe the persons who were responsible for the accident are afraid to reveal his whereabouts until he recovers from possible injuries. You'll see! Mr. Nestor will come back safe!"

And, somehow, though her mother was skeptical, Mary believed what Tom said.

The search was kept up, but without result, and Tom aided all he could. But there was not much he could do. The police and other authorities were at a total loss.

In the intervals of visiting Mary and her mother, and doing what he could for them, Tom worked on his new motor. He knew that he was on the right track and that all that was needed now was to make certain refinements and adjustments in the apparatus he had already constructed, so that it would operate more quietly.

"Absorbing the vibrations from the exhaust, caused by the exploded gases in the cylinders, does the trick," Tom told his father.

"But there is enormous pressure to overcome, Tom. You must be sure your muffler will stand the strain. Otherwise she is going to blow out a gasket some day, when you least expect it. Then the sudden resumption of pressure outside the cylinders is going to cause a change in the equilibrium, and you may turn turtle in the air."

"I've thought of that," said Tom. "At worst it can't be any more than looping the loop. But I'll make the muffler doubly strong."

"Better provide an auxiliary chamber to take care of part of the exhaust in case your main apparatus breaks," advised the older inventor, and Tom said he would. He did, too, for he valued his father's expert advice.

Meanwhile he was busy fitting one of his latest aeroplanes with the new motor. The motor he and Mr. Damon had used in their flight was one patched up from an old one. But now

Tom was working on a complete new one, made after his revised model, and in which the silencer was an integral part, instead of being built on.

While giving Mary and her mother all the assistance in his power, Tom still found time to work on his new, pet scheme. He had matters now where he did not fear any tampering with his plans, for he had filed away his papers in a safe place, and was making his new machine from memory.

"But if some one got in and had a look at the inside of your silencer he could see how it is constructed, couldn't he?" asked Ned Newton.

"Yes," assented Tom, "But they're not going to get in very easily. Koku sleeps in the experiment shop now, and my machine is there."

"Oh, well that explains your confidence. I feel sorry for the burglar who makes the attempt, once Koku wakes up. Heard anything more from those Universal people?"

"No, not directly. I understand they are working hard on some new type of plane for army use, but I haven't bothered my head about them. I'm too much occupied with my own affairs and trying to help Mary."

"Very strange about Mr. Nestor, isn't it?"

"Worse than strange," said Tom. "If this keeps on, and he isn't heard from, it will be tragic pretty soon."

"He must be held a prisoner somewhere," declared Ned.

"It begins to look that way," assented Tom. "Though who would have an object in that I can't understand. He had no enemies, as far as is known, and his business affairs were in excellent shape. Unless, as I said, the persons who ran him down are, through fear, keeping him hidden until he recovers, I can't imagine what has become of him."

"Well, it certainly is a puzzle," said Ned. And Tom agreed with his chum.

It was about a week after the disappearance of Mr. Nestor that Mr. Damon came over to see Tom.

"Bless my shoe laces, Tom!" exclaimed the eccentric man, "but you are as busy as ever." For he found the young inventor in the experiment shop, surrounded by a mass of papers and all sorts of mechanical devices.

"Yes, I'm working a little," said Tom. "But you are just in time. Come on out, I want to introduce you to Silent Sam."

"'Silent Sam!'" exclaimed Mr. Damon. "Have you been taking a new trip to the Land of Wonders? Have you brought back some new kind of servant?"

"Not exactly a servant," said Tom with a laugh, "though I hope Silent Sam will serve me well."

"'Silent Sam?' What does it mean? Is that a joke?" asked the puzzled Mr. Damon.

"I hope it doesn't turn out a joke," replied Tom. "But come on, I'll introduce you to him, Mr. Damon."

He led the way to one of the big hangars where his various machines of the air were housed. On the way Mr. Damon asked about news of Mr. Nestor, but was told there was none.

Tom Swift opened the big, swinging doors and pulled aside an enveloping canvas curtain. There stood revealed a big aeroplane, of somewhat new pattern, the wings gleaming like silver from the varnish that had been applied. In shape it was not unlike the machines already in use, except that the propellers were of somewhat different design.

The engine was mounted in front, and even with his slight knowledge of mechanics Mr. Damon could tell that it was exceedingly powerful. But it was certain devices attached to the engine that attracted his attention, for they were totally different from any on any other aeroplane, though they bore some resemblance to apparatus on the plane in which Tom and the eccentric man had made the night flight.

"Is this your new machine, Tom?" asked Mr. Damon.

"Yes."

"Well, I don't see anything of that fellow you spoke of—Silent Sam."

"This is Silent Sam," returned Tom, with a laugh. "I've named my new noiseless aeroplane—my Air Scout—I've named that Silent Sam. Wait until you hear it, or rather, don't hear it, and I think you'll agree with me. Silent Sam for Uncle Sam!"

"Good!" cried Mr. Damon. "Bless my dictionary, but that's a good name! Does it sail silently, Tom?"

"I'll let you judge presently. Silent Sam is all ready for his first trial, and I'll be glad to have you with me. Now, I'll just—"

Tom suddenly ceased speaking and held up a hand to enjoin silence. Then, while Mr. Damon watched, the young inventor began moving noiselessly toward the rear of the big shed, inside which was his new machine.

CHAPTER XVIII

SUSPICIONS

"Who's there?" suddenly called Tom, and in such a sharp voice that Mr. Damon started, ready as he was for something unusual.

There was no answer and Tom suddenly switched on all the lights in the shed. Up to then there had been only a few glowing—just enough for him to show the new Air Scout to his friend.

"Who's there?" asked Tom again, sharply.

"Bless my opera glasses, Tom!" cried Mr. Damon, "but are you seeing things?"

"No; but I'm hearing them," answered Tom with a short laugh. "Did you think you heard some one moving around near the rudders of Silent Sam, Mr. Damon?"

"No, I can't say that I did. Everything seems to me to be all right."

"Well, it doesn't to me," went on Tom grimly. "I think there is an intruder in this shed, though how any one could get in when the doors have been locked all day, is more than I can figure out. But I'm going to have a look."

"I'll help you," offered Mr. Damon, and, in the bright glare from many electric lights, the two began a search of the big hangar where the new craft was kept.

But though the young inventor and his friend went around to the rear of the aeroplane, walking in opposite directions, they saw no one, nor did any one try to escape past them.

"And yet I was sure I heard some one in here," declared Tom, when a search had revealed nothing. "It sounded as if some one were scuffling softly about in rubber-soled shoes, trying to hide."

"Bless my suspenders!" cried Mr. Damon, "who do you think it could have been, Tom?"

"Who else but some spy trying to get possession of my secrets?" was the answer. "But I guess I was too quick for them. They couldn't learn much from looking at the outside of my muffler, and it hasn't been disturbed, as far as I can see."

"Who would want to gain a knowledge of it in that unlawful way?" asked Mr. Damon.

"Perhaps some of the Universal crowd. They may have been disappointed in perfecting a silent motor themselves, and think stealing my idea would be the easiest way out of it."

"Do they know you are working on such a model as this Silent Sam of yours, Tom?"

"Yes, I imagine they do. One of the firm members, as you recall, overheard something, I think, that gave them a hint as to what my plans were, though, thanks to the time I fooled the spy, they haven't any real data to go by, I believe."

"Let us hope not," said Mr. Damon.

Tom and he made a thorough search of the big shed, but found no one, nor was there any trace of an intruder. Tom notified Jackson, who, in turn, told the guards and watchmen to be on the lookout for any suspicious strangers, but none was seen in the vicinity of the Swift works.

"Well, everything seems to be all right, so we'll have the test," remarked Tom, after a further search of the premises. "Now, Mr. Damon, if all goes as I hope you will see what my new machine can do. Strain your ears for a sound, and let me know how much you hear."

His men helping him, Tom started the new motor which was tried for the first time attached to the new craft. No flight was to be made yet, the motor being tested as though on the block, though, in reality, the craft was ready for instant flight if need be.

Slowly the great propellers began to revolve, and then Tom, taking his place in the cockpit, turned on more power. The new craft—Silent Sam—was made fast so it could not progress even though the propellers revolved at high speed.

"I'm not sending her to the limit," said Tom to his friend, as the young inventor throttled down the motor. "If I did I'd tear her loose from the holding blocks."

"Her!" cried Mr. Damon. "Bless my typewriter, Tom! but I thought Silent Sam was a gentleman aeroplane.

"So he is!" laughed the young man, frankly. "I forgot about 'Silent Sam.' Guess I'll have to say 'him' instead of 'her,' though the latter sounds more natural. Anyhow what do you think?"

"I think it's wonderful!" exclaimed Mr. Damon. "There the motor is, going at almost full speed, and I can hardly hear a thing. You can the easier believe that when I say that I can hear you talk perfectly well. And I guess you hear me, don't you?"

"Yes," replied Tom. "And we don't have to shout, either. This is the best test ever! I think everything is a success."

"Are you going to take her aloft, Tom?" the eccentric man went on.

"Yes, now that I'm sure the engine is all right. Will you go for a flight with me?"

"I certainly will! I only wish we could find him, though. I'd go with a better heart."

"Oh! Mr. Nestor?"

"Yes, I can't imagine what has become of him. It is almost as if the earth had opened and swallowed him. His disappearance is a great mystery."

"It surely is," agreed Tom. "Can't seem to get any trace of him. But if we hear another cry for help, when we have to land, you can make up your mind I'll investigate more quickly than I did at first."

"I agree with you," said Mr. Damon.

It was nearly evening then, and until it was dark enough for his flight Tom spent the time tuning up the engine and seeing that all was in readiness for the latest test. He had decided not to go aloft while it was light enough for curiosity seekers to note the flight.

Tom rather wished Mary Nestor might have a sail with him in his latest improved silent Air Scout, but the girl was too much occupied at home and in trying to find some trace of her father.

Tom, his father, and Mr. Damon had helped all they could, but there were no results. A private detective had been engaged, but he had no more of a clew than the regular police.

At last it was dark enough for the flight, and Tom and Mr. Damon took their places in the machine. Once more the propellers were turned around, and when the compression had been made, and the spark switched on, around spun the big wooden blades, and the great craft moved over the grass.

On and on and up and up sailed Tom and Mr. Damon, and as they left behind them the shops and the Swift homestead, the two passengers were aware of their almost silent flight. The big aeroplane, the exhaust of which, ordinarily, would have nearly deafened them, was now as silent as a bird.

"Silent Sam for Uncle Sam!" cried Tom in delight, as he went on faster. "I'm sure the government ought to be glad to get this plane for air scout work. It's a success! A great success!"

"Yes, so it is!" agreed Mr. Damon. "You do well to speak of it so, Tom."

For, modest as the young inventor was, he felt, in justice to himself, that he must acknowledge the fact that his craft was a success. For it rose and sailed almost as silently as a bat, and a few hundred feet away no one, not seeing it, would have believed a big aeroplane was in motion.

Tom and Mr. Damon flew about twenty miles at a swift pace, and all the fault Tom had to find was that the machine was not as steady in flight as she should have been.

"But I can remedy that with the use of some of dad's gyroscope stabilizers," he told Mr. Damon.

They returned to the hangar safely, and the first trip of the new Silent Sam was an assured success.

It was the following day, when Tom was busy in the machine shop installing the gyroscopes spoken of, that Jackson came to tell him there was a visitor to see him.

"Who is it?" asked the young inventor.

"Mr. Gale of the Universal Company," was the answer.

"I don't want to see him!" declared Tom quickly. "I have nothing to say to him after his clumsy threats."

"He seems very much in earnest," said Jackson. "Better see him, if only for a minute or so."

"All right, I will," assented Tom. "Show him in."

Mr. Gale, as blusteringly bluff as ever, entered the shop. Tom had carefully put away all papers and models, as well as the finished machines, so he had no fear that his visitor might discover some secret.

"Oh, Mr. Swift!" began the president of the Universal Company, when he met the young inventor, "I wish to assure you that what has been done was entirely without our knowledge.

And, though this man may have acted as our agent at one time, we repudiate any acts of his that might—"

"What are you talking about?" asked Tom in surprise. "Have I been so impolite as to sleep during part of your talk? I don't understand what you are driving at."

"Oh, I thought you did," said Gale, and he showed surprise. "I understood that the man who—"

"Do you mean there was some one here in the shed last night?" cried the young inventor suddenly, all his suspicions aroused.

"Some one here last night?" repeated Mr. Gale. "No, I don't refer to last night. But perhaps I am making a mistake. I—er—I—"

"Some one is making a mistake!" said Tom significantly.

CHAPTER XIX

ANOTHER FLIGHT

For perhaps a quarter of a minute Tom Swift and the president of the Universal Flying Machine Company of New York sat staring at one another. Mr. Gale's face wore a puzzled expression, and so did Tom's. And, after the last remark of the young inventor, the man who had called to see him said:

"Well, perhaps we are talking at cross purposes. I don't blame you for not feeling very friendly toward us, and if I had had my way that last correspondence with you would never have left our office."

"It wasn't very business-like," said Tom dryly, referring to the veiled threats when he had refused to sell his services to the rival company.

"I realize that," said Mr. Gale. "But we have some peculiar men working for us, and sometimes there is so much to do, so many possibilities of which to take advantage, that we may get a little off our balance. But what I called for was not to renew our offer to you. I understand that is definitely settled."

"As far as I am concerned, it is," said Tom, as his caller seemed to want an answer.

"Yes. Well, then, what I called to say was that if you are thinking of taking any legal action against us because of the action of that man Lydane, I wish to state that he had absolutely no authority to—"

"Excuse me!" broke in Tom, "but by Lydane do you mean the man who also posed as Bower, the spy?"

"No, I do not. Though I regret to say that Bower once worked for us. He, too, had no authority to come here and get a position. He was still in our service when he did that."

"So I have suspected," said Tom. "I realize now that he was a spy, who came here to try to find out for you some of my secrets."

"Not with my permission!" exclaimed Mr. Gale. "I was against that from the first and I came to tell you so. But Bower really did you no harm."

"No, he didn't get the chance!" chuckled Tom. "Nor did that other spy—the one with the gold tooth. I wonder how he liked our mud hole?"

"He was Lydane," said Mr. Gale. "It is about him I came."

"You might have saved yourself the trouble," returned Tom. "I don't wish to discuss him."

"But I wish to make sure," said Mr. Gale, "that what he has done will not come back on us. We repudiate him entirely. His methods we can not countenance. He is too daring—"

"Oh, don't worry!" interrupted Tom. "He hasn't done anything to me—he didn't get the chance, as I guess he's told you. You needn't apologize on his account. He did me no harm, and—"

"But I understood from him that—"

"Now I don't want to seem impolite!" broke in Tom, "nor do I want to take pattern after some of your company's acts, if not your own. But I am very busy. I have an important test to make for the government, and my time is fully occupied. I am afraid I shall have to bid you good-morning and—"

"But won't you give me a chance to—" began the president.

"Now, the less we discuss this matter the better!" interrupted Tom. "Lydane, as you call the man with the gold tooth didn't really do anything to me nor any great harm to any of my possessions, as far as I can learn. His career is a closed book—a book with muddy covers!" and the young inventor laughed.

"Oh, well, if you look at it that way, there is nothing further for me to say," said Mr. Gale stiffly. "I understood— But hasn't my partner, Mr. Ware, seen you?" he asked Tom quickly.

"No. And I don't care to see him."

"Oh, then that accounts for it," was the quick answer. "Well, if you regard the matter as closed I suppose we should also. We are not to blame for what Lydane does when he is no longer in our employ, and we repudiate anything he may do, or may have done."

This struck Tom, afterward, as being rather a queer remark, but he did not think so at the time.

The truth was that the young inventor wished very much to try out a new device on his noiseless aeroplane and wanted to get rid of Mr. Gale before doing so. So he did not pay as much attention to the remarks of the president as, otherwise, he might have done.

It was not until after Mr. Gale had taken his leave and Tom had finished the particular work on which he was engaged when the president of the rival company came in, that the young man did some hard thinking. And this thinking was done after he had received a telephone call from Mary Nestor, asking, if by any chance, he had heard anything like a clew as to the whereabouts of her father.

Tom had been obliged to tell her that he had not. Everything possible was being done to find the missing man but he had disappeared as completely as though he had ridden on his bicycle into the crater of some extinct volcano on the meadow, and had fallen to the bottom.

An effort was made to trace him through an automobile association which had a large membership. That is, the members were asked to make inquiries to ascertain, if possible, whether any one had heard of an unreported accident—one in which Mr. Nestor might have been carried away by persons who accidently ran him down.

But this came to naught, and the police and other authorities were at a loss how farther to proceed. It was a theory in some quarters that Mr. Nestor was perfectly safe, but that he was out of his mind, and was either wandering around, not knowing who he was, or was, in this condition, detained somewhere, the persons having him in charge not realizing that he was the missing man so widely sought.

This belief was a relief to Mrs. Nestor and Mary in many ways for it prevented them from giving way to the fear that Mr. Nestor was dead. That he was alive was Tom Swift's firm opinion, and he was doing all he could to prove it.

It was not until the day after the visit of Mr. Gale that Tom, having concluded some intricate calculations about the strength of cylinder valves, uttered an exclamation.

"I wonder if he could have meant that?" cried the young inventor. "I wonder if he could have meant that? I must find out at once! Queer I didn't think of that before!"

He put in a long distance call to New York, asking to speak to Mr. Gale. But when, eventually, he was connected with the office of the Universal Flying Machine Company he was told that Mr. Gale and Mr. Ware had sailed for France that day, going over as government representatives to investigate aeroplane motors. Gale's visit to Tom had been just previous to taking the boat, it was said.

"This is tough luck!" mused Tom, his suspicions doubly aroused now. "I can't let this rest here! I've got to get after it! As soon as I make this final test, and invite Uncle Sam's experts out to see how my noiseless motor works, I'll get after Gale and

Ware if I have to follow them to the battlefields of France! I wonder if it was that he was hinting at all the while! I begin to believe it was!"

Tom Swift had decided on another flight for his new craft before he would let the government experts see it.

"Silent Sam must do his very best work for Uncle Sam before I turn him over," said the young inventor.

"And after this flight I'll offer the machine to the government, and then devote all my time to finding Mr. Nestor," said Tom. "I'd do it now, but private matters, however deeply they affect us, must be put aside to help win the war. But this will end my inventive work until after Mr. Nestor is found—if he's alive."

Preparations for the test flight went on apace, and one afternoon Tom and Jackson took their places in the big, new aeroplane. He no longer feared daylight crowds in case of an accident. They made a good start, and the motor was so quiet that as Tom passed over his own plant the men working in the yard, who did not know of the flight, did not look up to see what was going on. They could not hear the engine.

"I think we've got everything just as we want it, Jackson," said Tom, much pleased.

"I believe you," answered the mechanician. "It couldn't be better. Now if—"

And at that moment there came a loud explosion, and Silent Sam began drifting rapidly toward the earth, as falls a bird with a broken wing.

CHAPTER XX

QUEER MARKS

"What happened?" cried Jackson to Tom, as he leaned forward in his seat which was in the rear of the young inventor's.

"Don't know, exactly," was the answer, as Tom quickly shifted the rudders to correct the slanting fall of his craft. "Sounded as though there was a tremendous back-fire, or else the muffler blew up. The engine is dead."

"Can you take her down safely?"

"Oh, yes, I guess so. She's a bit out of control, but the stabilizer will keep her on a level keel. Good thing we installed it."

"You're right!" said Jackson.

Now they were falling earthward with great rapidity, but, thanks to the gyroscope stabilizer, the "side-slipping," than which there is no motion more dreaded by an aviator, had nearly ceased. The craft was volplaning down as it ought, and Tom had it under as perfect control as was possible under the circumstances.

"We'll get down all right if something else doesn't happen," he said to Jackson, with grim humor.

"Well, let's hope that it won't," said the mechanic. "We're a good distance up yet."

They were, as a matter of fact, for the explosion, or whatever had happened to the craft, had occurred at a height of over two miles, and they at once began falling. As yet Tom Swift was unaware of the exact nature of the accident or its cause. All he knew was that there had been a big noise and that the engine had stopped working. He could not see the silencer from where he sat, as it was constructed on the underside of the motor, but he had an idea that the same sort of mishap had occurred as on the occasion when the test machine had sailed through the roof of his workshop.

"But, luckily, this wasn't as bad," mused Tom. "Anyhow the motor is out of business."

And this was very evident. The young inventor had tried to start the apparatus after its stoppage by the explosion, but it had not responded to his efforts, and then he had desisted, fearing to cause some further damage, or, perhaps, endanger his own life and that of Jackson.

Down, down swept Silent Sam—doubly silent now, and Tom began looking about for a good place to make a landing. This was nothing new for either him or his mechanician, and they accepted the outcome as a matter of course.

"Not a very lively place down there," remarked Jackson, as he looked over the side of the cockpit.

"If we have to depend for help on any one down there, I guess we'll be a long time waiting," agreed Tom. They were about to land in a very lonely spot. It was one he had never before visited, though he knew it could not be much more than twenty miles from his own home, as they had not flown much farther than that distance.

But, somehow or other, Tom had not visited this particular section, and knew nothing of it. He saw below him, as Jackson had seen, a lonely stretch of country—a big field, once a woodlot, evidently, as scattered about were some stumps and some second growth trees. There were also a number of evergreens—Christmas trees Jackson called them. And this was the only open place for miles, the surrounding country being a densely wooded one. There did not appear to be a house or other building in sight where they might seek help.

"But maybe we can make the repairs ourselves and keep on," the lad thought.

With practiced eye he picked out a smooth, grassy, level spot, in the midst of scattered evergreen trees, and there Tom Swift skillfully brought his Air Scout to rest. With a gentle thud the rubber-tired wheels struck the Earth, rolled along a little distance, and then called to a stop.

Hardly had the aeroplane ceased moving when Tom and his companion jumped out and began eagerly to examine the machinery to see the extent of damage.

"I thought so!" Tom exclaimed. "The silencer cracked under the strain. Those exhaust gases have more pressure that I believed possible. I increased the margin of safety on this muffler, too. But she's cracked, and I can't use the machine until I put on a new one. Good thing I didn't ask for a government inspection until after this trial flight."

"That's so," agreed Jackson. "But can't you patch it up, or go on without a muffler, so we can get back home?"

"I'm afraid not," Tom answered. "You see I removed all the old exhaust pipe fittings when I put on my new silencer. Now if I took off my attachment there wouldn't be anything to carry off the discharged gases, and they'd form a regular cloud about us. We couldn't stand it without gas masks, such as they use in the trenches, and we haven't any of those with us."

"That's right," agreed Jackson. "Well, what do you want to do? Have me stay here and guard the machine while you go for help? Or shall I go?"

"I don't know why we both can't go," said Tom. "There is no use trying to patch up this machine here. I'll have to send a truck after it, and dismantle it before I can get it home.

"As for either of us staying here on guard, I don't quite see the need of that. This looks like the jumping-off place to me. I don't believe there's a native within miles. I didn't see any houses as we came down, and I think Silent Sam will be perfectly safe here. No one can run off with him, anyhow. He'd be as hard to start as an automobile with all four wheels gone. Let's leave it here and both walk back."

"All right," agreed Jackson. "That suits me. Might as well leave our togs here, too. It will be easier walking without them," and he began taking off the fur-lined suit, his cap, and his goggles, such as he and Tom wore against the piercing cold of the upper regions.

"We can stuff them in the cockpit and leave them," went on the mechanician, as he divested himself of his garments. As he stowed them away in his seat he gave one more look at the broken muffler. As Tom Swift said, his new silencer had literally blown up, a large piece having been torn from the gas chamber.

Something that Jackson saw caused him to utter an exclamation that brought Tom Swift to his side.

"What is it?" asked the young inventor.

"Look!" was the answer. "See! Just at the edge of that break! It's been filed to make the metal thinner there than anywhere else. You didn't do that, did you?"

"I should say not!" cried Tom. "Why, to file there would mean to weaken the whole structure."

"And that's exactly what's happened!" declared Jackson, as he gave another look. "Some one has filed this nearly through —leaving only a thin metal skin, and when the gas pressure became too much it blew out. That's what happened!"

Tom Swift made a quick but thorough examination.

"You're right, Jackson!" he exclaimed. "That was filed deliberately to cause the accident. And it must have been done lately, for I carefully inspected the silencer when I put it on, and it was in perfect order. There's been spy work here. Some one got into the hangar and filed that casing. Then the accumulated pressure of the gases did the rest."

"As sure as you're alive!" agreed Jackson. "Maybe that's what Gale did when he called."

"No," returned Tom, shaking his head, "he didn't get a chance to do anything like that. I watched him all the while. But perhaps this is what he referred to when he said he and his company would repudiate any act of that spy with the gold tooth—Lydane, so Gale said his name was. Maybe that's what Lydane did."

"He was capable of it," agreed the mechanic, "but he couldn't have done it that time you tripped him into the mud puddle. This silencer wasn't built then."

"No, you're right," assented Tom. "Then he must have been around since, doing some of his tricky work!"

"I don't see how that could have been," said Jackson slowly. "We've kept a very careful watch, and your shop has been specially guarded."

"I know it has," said Tom. "There couldn't much get past Koku; but some one seems to have done it, or else how could that filing have been done?"

Jackson shook his head. The problem was too much for him. He looked carefully at the exploded and broken silencer, and Tom, too, gave it a critical eye. There was no doubt but that it had been filed in several places to weaken the structure of the metal.

"When did you last see that it was in perfect condition?" asked Jackson.

Tom named a certain date.

"That was just before Gale called," observed the mechanician. "He might have known of it."

"I wish I'd known of it at the time," said Tom savagely. "He wouldn't have gotten away as easily as he did. Well, there's no use standing here talking about it. Let's get back to civilization and we'll send back one of the trucks. Luckily I have another silencer I can put on for the government test. This one will never be of any more use, though I may be able to save some of the valves and baffle plates."

Slowly they turned from the disabled aeroplane and started to look for a path that would lead them out of the lonely place. Tom as the first to strike what seemed to be a cow path, or perhaps what had been a road into the wood lot in the early days.

As he tramped along it, followed by Jackson, the young inventor suddenly stopped, as he came to a sandy place, and, stooping over, looked intently at some queer marks in the soil.

"What is it?" asked the mechanician.

"Looks like the marks of an automobile," said Tom slowly. "And I was just trying to remember where I'd seen marks like these before."

CHAPTER XXI

THE DESERTED CABIN

For several seconds the young inventor remained bending over the queer marks in that little sandy path of the lonely field in the midst of the silent woods. Jackson watched him curiously, and then Tom straightened up, exclaiming as he did so:

"I have it! Now I know where it was! I saw marks like these the night Mr. Nestor disappeared. Mr. Damon and I noticed the marks in the dust on the road the time we made the forced landing the first night we tried out the silent motor. That's it! They are the same marks! I'm sure of it!"

"I wouldn't go so far as to say that," said Jackson slowly. He was more deliberate than Tom Swift, a fact for which the young inventor was often glad, as it saved him from impulsive mistakes.

"This may not be the same auto," went on the mechanician. "I'll admit I never saw square tire marks like those before. Most of the usual ones are circular, diamond-shape or oblong. Some tire manufacturer must have tried a new stunt. But as for saying these marks were made by the same machine you saw evidences of the night Mr. Nestor disappeared, why, that's going a little too far, Tom."

"Yes, I suppose it is," admitted the young inventor. "But it's a clew worth following. Maybe Mr. Nestor has been brought to some lonely place like this, and is being held."

"Why would any one want to do that?" asked Jackson. "He had no enemies."

"Well, perhaps those who ran him down and injured him are afraid to let him go for fear he will prosecute them and ask for heavy damages," suggested Tom. "They may be holding him a captive until he gets well, and aim on treating him so nicely that he won't bring suit."

"That's a pretty far-fetched theory," said the mechanician as he carefully looked at the tracks. "But of course it may be true. Anyhow, these tire marks are rather recent, I should say, and they are made by a new tire. Do you think we can follow them?"

"I'm going to try!" declared Tom. "The only trouble is we can't tell whether it was going or coming—that is we don't know which way to go."

"That's so," agreed his companion. "And so the only thing to do is to travel a bit both ways. The path, or road, or whatever you call it, is plainly enough marked here, though you can't always pick out the tire marks. They show only on bare ground. The grass doesn't leave any tracks that we can see, though doubtless they are there.

"But as for thinking this car is the same one the marks of which you saw on the lonely moor, the night you heard the call for help—that's going too far, Tom Swift."

"Yes, I realize that. Of course there must be more than one car with tires which have square protuberances. But it's worth taking a chance on—following this clew."

"Oh, sure!" agreed Jackson.

"The only question is, then, which way to go," returned Tom.

They settled that, arbitrarily enough, by going on in the direction they had started after leaving the stranded airship. They followed a half-defined path, and were rewarded by getting occasional glimpses on bare ground of the odd tire marks.

Through a devious winding way, now hidden amid a lane of trees, and again cutting across an open space, the path led. They saw the marks often enough to make sure they were on the right trail, and in one place they saw several different patches of the odd marks.

They went on perhaps half a mile more, when they came to a lonely road and saw where the car had turned from that into the wood-lot, as Tom called the place where his craft had settled down.

"Look!" cried the young inventor to Jackson. "They've been here more than once, and have gone along the road in both directions. They seem to have used this turning into the lot as a sort of stopping place."

This was plain enough from an examination of the marks in the sandy soil of the road, which was one not often used. The automobile with the queer, square marks on the tires had turned into the lot, coming and going in both directions.

"This settles it!" cried Tom, when he finished making an examination. "There's something farther back in this lot that we've got to see. This auto has been coming and going, and we should have followed the tracks the other way from the point where we first saw them, instead of coming this way."

"Except that we've learned the place of departure," suggested Jackson. "Evidently the wood-lot is a blind alley. The car goes in, but it can come out only just at this point, or, at least, it does."

"That's right!" agreed Tom. "Now the thing to do is to follow our track back to where we started. There must be some place where the car went to—some headquarters, or meeting place with some one, farther back in the lot. If we can only follow the trail back as well as we did coming, we may find out something."

"Well, let's try, anyhow," suggested Jackson.

They had no difficulty in making their way back to the spot where they had first seen the queer marks. But from then on their task was not so easy. For sandy or bare patches of earth were not frequent, and they had to depend on these to give them direction, for the road was overgrown and not well defined.

Often they would search about for some time after leaving one patch of the marks before they found another that would justify them in keeping on.

"They have headquarters, or a rendezvous, somewhere back in this lot!" declared Tom, as they hurried on. "I think we're on the track of a mystery."

"Unless it turns out that some farmer has treated himself to an auto with new tires of square tread, and is hauling wood," said Jackson. "It may turn out that way."

"Yes, it may," agreed Tom. "But, taking everything into consideration, I think we're on the verge of finding out something. Even if we do discover that the owner of this auto is only hauling wood, he may be able to help us to a clew as to the whereabouts of Mr. Nestor."

"How?"

"Well, maybe he was in his machine on the moor the night the call for help came. He may even have aided to carry Mr. Nestor away. And if he doesn't know a thing about it—which, of course, is possible—the man who bought these queer tires can tell us who makes them, or who deals in them, and we can find out what autoists around here have their cars equipped with this odd tread."

"Yes," agreed Jackson, "that can be done."

And so they kept on, scouting here and there to either side

of the half-defined path, until they were far back from the spot where they had left the Air Scout.

"We don't appear to be getting any warmer, as the children say," remarked Jackson, as he straightened up and looked about, for his back ached from so much stooping over to look for the odd marks.

"We haven't seen anything yet, I'll admit," said Tom. "But it won't be dark for another hour or so, and I vote that we keep on."

"Oh, I wasn't thinking of giving up!" exclaimed Jackson. "If there's anything here—at the end of the route, as you might say—we'll find it. Only I hope it doesn't turn out to be just a wood pile, from which some farmer has been hauling logs."

"That would be a disappointment," assented Tom.

The day was waning, and they realized that they ought not to spend too much time on what might turn out to be a wild goose chase. They were in a lonely neighborhood, and while they were not at all apprehensive of danger, they felt it would be best to get to shelter before dark.

"We'll want to send word to Mr. Swift that we're all right."

"Yes," said Tom, "I'd like to get to a place where I can telephone to him or Mrs. Baggert. Well, if we don't find something pretty soon we'll have to turn back. I must complete work on the new motor, for if I'm to offer it to Uncle Sam for air scout purposes, the sooner I can do so the better. Things are getting pretty hot over in Europe, and if ever the United States needed aircraft on the western front they need them now. I want to help all I can, and I also want to help Mary—you understand —Miss Nestor."

"I understand," said Jackson simply. "I only hope you can help her. But I'm afraid—this may turn out to be nothing—following these marks, you know."

"And yet," said Tom slowly, "it would be strange if it was only a coincidence—the two tire marks being the same—the night Mr. Nestor disappeared and now."

And so they kept on, hoping.

The half-defined path through the wood-lot led them in a series of turns and twists, and it extended through a dense patch of woods, growing thickly, where it was so dark that it seemed as if night had fallen.

"We can't spend much more time here," said Tom. "If we don't find something in the next half mile we'll go back and take up the search to-morrow. I'm going to find out what's at the end of this road—even if it's only a wood pile."

For ten minutes more the two went on, making sure, by occasional glimpses at the marks, that they were on the right track. Then, suddenly, they saw something which made them feel sure they had reached their goal.

In a clearing among the trees was a little cabin—a shack of logs—and from the appearance it was deserted. There was not a sign of life around.

CHAPTER XXII

CLEWS AT LAST

For a moment, at sight of the deserted cabin, staring at Tom and his friend, as it were, from its hiding place amid the trees, the young inventor and his companion did not move. They just stood looking at the place.

"Well," said Tom, at length, "we found it, didn't we?"

"We found something anyhow," agreed Jackson. "Whether it amounts to anything or not, we've got to see."

"Come on!" cried Tom, impulsively. "I'm going to see what's there."

"There doesn't appear to be much of anything," said Jackson, as he looked toward the lonely cabin with critical eyes. "I should say that place hadn't been used, even as a chicken coop, in a long while."

"We can soon tell!" exclaimed Tom, striding forward.

"Wait just a minute!" cried his companion, catching him by the coat. "Don't be in such a hurry."

"Why not?" asked Tom. "There isn't any danger, is there?"

"I don't know about that. There's no telling who may be hidden in that cabin, in spite of its deserted appearance. And though there aren't any 'No Trespass' signs up, it may be that we wouldn't be welcome. If there are some tramps there, which is possible, they might take a notion to shoot at us first and ask questions as to our peaceable intentions afterward—when it would be too late."

"Nonsense!" exclaimed Tom. "There aren't any tramps there

and, if there were, they wouldn't dare shoot. I'm going to see what the mystery is—if there is one."

But there was no sign of life, and, taking this as an indication that their advance would not be disputed, Jackson followed Tom. The latter advanced until he could take in all the details of the shack. It was made of logs, and once had been chinked with mud or clay. Some of this had fallen out, leaving spaces between the tree trunks.

"It wasn't a bad little shack at one time," decided Tom. "Maybe it was a place where some one camped out during the summer. But it hasn't been used of late. I never knew there was such a place around here, and I thought I knew this locality pretty well."

"I never heard of it, either," said Jackson. "Let's give a shout and see if there's any one around. They may be asleep. Hello, there!" he called in sufficiently vigorous tones to have awakened an ordinary sleeper.

Put there was no answer, and as the shadows of the night began to fall, the place took on a most lonely aspect.

"Let's go up and knock—or go in if the door's open," suggested Tom. "We can't lose any more time, if we're to get out of here before night."

"Go ahead," said Jackson, and together they went to the cabin door.

"Locked!" exclaimed Tom, as he saw a padlock attached to a chain. It appeared to be fastened through two staples, driven one into the door and the other into the jamb, at right angles to one another and overlapping.

"Knock!" suggested Jackson. But when Tom had done so, and there was no answer, the machinist took hold of the lock. To his own surprise and that of Tom, one of the staples pulled out and the door swung open. The place had evidently been forced before, and the lock had not been opened by a key. The staple had been pulled out and replaced loosely in the holes.

For a moment nothing could be made out in the dark interior of the shack. But as their eyes became used to the gloom, Tom and his companion were able to see that the shack consisted of two rooms.

In the first one there was a rusty stove, a table, and some chairs, and it was evident, from pans and skillets hanging on the wall, as well as from a small cupboard built on one side, that this was the kitchen and living room combined.

"Anybody here?" cried Tom, as he stepped inside.

Only a dull echo answered.

The two could now see where a door gave entrance to an inner room, and this, a quick glance showed, was the sleeping apartment, two bunks being built on the side walls.

"Well, somebody had it pretty comfortable here," decided Tom, as he looked around. "They've been cooking and sleeping here, and not so very long ago, either. It wouldn't be such a bad place if it was cleaned out."

"That's right," agreed Jackson. "Wouldn't mind camping here myself, if there was any fishing near."

"The river can't be far away," suggested Tom. "And now let's see what we can find, and see if we can get a line on who has been here. But first we'll let in a little light."

He opened a window in the sleeping room, and pushed back the heavy plank shutter that had been closed. When the light entered it was seen that both bunks bore evidence of having been lately slept in. The blankets were tossed back, as if the occupants had risen, and in the outer room, on the stove, were signs that indicated a meal had been served not many days gone by.

"Now," observed Tom musingly, as he wandered about the

place, "if we could only find out who owns this, and who has been here lately—"

Jackson stooped over, and, thrusting aside an end of the blankets that trailed on the floor from one of the bunks, picked up something.

"What is it?" asked Tom.

"Looks like a leather pocketbook," was the answer. "That's what it is," the mechanic went on, as he held the object to the light. "It's a wallet."

"Let me see it!" exclaimed Tom quickly. He took the wallet from the hands of Jackson. Then the young inventor uttered a cry. "A clew at last!" he exclaimed. "A clew at last! Mr. Nestor has been in this cabin!"

"How do you know?" asked Jackson quickly.

"This is his wallet," said Tom excitedly. "I've often seen him have it. In fact he had it with him on Earthquake Island, the time I sent the wireless message for help. I saw it several times then. He kept in it what few papers he had saved from the wreck. And I've seen it often enough since. That's Mr. Nestor's wallet all right. Besides, if you want any other evidence—look!" He opened the leather flaps and showed Jackson on one, stamped in gold letters, the name of Mary's father.

"Well, what do you make of it, Tom?" asked the mechanician, as he finished his examination of the wallet. "What does it mean? The pocket-book is empty and that—"

"Might mean almost anything," completed Tom. "But it's a clew all right! He's been here, and I'm pretty certain he was brought here in the auto with the odd tires—the one Mr. Damon and I saw traces of the night we heard the cries for help."

"But that doesn't help us now," said Jackson. "The point is to find out how lately Mr. Nestor was here, and what has happened to him since. There isn't anything in the wallet, is there?"

"Nothing," answered Tom, making a careful examination so as to be sure. "It's as empty as a last year's bird nest. He's been robbed—that's what has happened to Mr. Nestor. He was waylaid that night, instead of being run down as I thought—waylaid and robbed and then his body was brought here."

"There you go again, Tom! Jumping to conclusions!" said Jackson, with a friendly smile, and with the familiarity of an old and valued helper. "Maybe he's in perfectly good health. Just because you found his empty wallet doesn't argue that your friend is in serious trouble. He may have dropped this on the road and some one picked it up. I'll admit they may have taken whatever was in it, but that doesn't prove anything. The thing for us to do is to find out who knows about this shack; who owns it, on whose land it is, and whether any one has been seen here lately."

"They've been here lately whether they've been seen or not," said Tom positively. "There are the auto tracks. It rained two days ago, and the tracks were made since. Mr. Nestor must have been here within two days."

"He may or may not," said Jackson. "Say, rather, that some one was here and left his wallet after him. Now see if we can find other clews!"

They looked about in the fast fading light, but at first could discover nothing more than evidences that three or four persons had been living in the shack and at some recent date—probably within a day or two.

They had had their meals there and had slept there. But this seemed to be all that could be established, other than that Mr. Nestor's wallet was there, stripped of its contents.

Tom was looking through the closet, from which a frightened chipmunk sprang as he opened the door. There were the remains of some food, which accounted for the presence of the little striped animal. And, as Tom poked about, his hand came in contact with something wrapped in paper on an upper shelf. It was something that clinked metallicly.

"What's that?" asked Jackson. "Knives, or some other weapons?"

"Neither," answered Tom. "It's a couple of files, and they've been used lately. I can see something in the grooves yet and—"

Suddenly Tom ceased speaking and drew from his pocket a small but powerful magnifying glass. Through this he looked at one of the files, taking it out in front of the shack where the light was better.

"I thought so!" he cried. "Look here, Jackson!"

"What is it?"

"Another clew!" answered Tom.

CHAPTER XXIII

THE GOVERNMENT TEST

For a moment Jackson thought Tom had discovered a clew to, or evidences of, some crime. He had an unpleasant suspicion, for an instant, that there was blood on the files, and that it might prove to be the blood of Mr. Nestor.

But the satisfaction that showed on Tom's face did not seem to indicate such dire possibilities as these.

"What is it?" asked Jackson, unable to guess at what Tom was looking through the powerful glass. "What do you see?"

"Metal filings on the grooves of these files," said the young inventor. "And, unless I'm greatly mistaken, the particles of filings are from the case of my aircraft silencer!"

"What!" cried the machinist. "Do you mean those are the files used in weakening the outer case of your new machine, so that it burst a little while ago?"

"That's what I think," answered Tom. "I know it sounds pretty far-fetched," he went on. "But take a look for yourself. If those particles on, the files aren't exactly of the same color and texture as the material of which the silencer case is made, I'll never build another machine."

Jackson peered through the powerful glass moving out a little farther from the shack, so as to get the best light possible on the subject of his examination. It was fast getting dark, but there was enough glow in the western sky for his purpose.

"Am I right?" asked Tom.

"You're right!" declared his helper. "This is exactly the same metal as that of which your silencer case is made. It's a peculiar mixture of aluminum and vanadium steel. I never knew it used in any shop but yours, and these filings are certainly of that metal. It would seem, Tom, that these were the files used to cut a crease in the case of your silencer to weaken it so it would burst."

"My idea exactly!" cried Tom. "The spy, who got into my shop in some undiscovered manner, did his work and then fled here to hide. He left his files behind. Mr. Nestor must have been here, either before or after. No, I'll not say that, either. Finding his wallet here doesn't prove that he was here. It might have been brought here by one of the spies and dropped. But I'm sure we're on the track of the men who damaged my airship, as well as those who know something of the mystery of Mr. Nestor."

"I agree with you," said Jackson. "Of course there's a possibility that the same peculiar metal you used in your silencer case may have been used in some other machine shop, and these files may have come from there, and have been employed in perfectly regular work. But the chances are—"

"There's only one way to make sure," said Tom. "Let's take the files with us and see if they fit in the grooves where the break came. We'll take these back to where we left the Air Scout," and he clinked the files he held.

"We can just about make it before it gets black dark," returned Jackson. "But that won't give us any more time to look around here," and he indicated the hut.

"I fancy we've seen all there is to see here," said Tom. "Mr. Nestor isn't here, and whether he was or not is a question. Anyhow, some one was here who had something to do with him after his disappearance, I'm positive of that. And I'm sure some one was here who damaged my airship. Now we'll run down both those clews, find out who owns this place, who has been using it, and all we can along that line. So, if you're ready, let's travel."

The two set out to make their way back to where they had left the stranded airship. It was fast becoming dark, but they could hurry along with more speed now, as they did not have to stop to look for the marks of the peculiar automobile tires. They had noticed the path along which they had traveled, and in half the time they had spent coming they were back where the Air Scout rested undisturbed in the meadow amid the trees.

Making sure that, as far as they could tell, no one had visited the craft since they had left it, Tom and Jackson compared the file marks on what was left of the broken silencer case with the files they had found in the hut. They used a small, but powerful electric lamp to aid them in this examination, as it was too dark to see otherwise, and what they saw caused the young inventor to exclaim:

"That settles it! These were the files used!"

"That's right!" agreed his assistant. "You've called the turn, Tom. The next thing to do is to find who connects with the files."

"Yes. To do that and find Mr. Nestor," said Tom. "We have plenty of work ahead of us. But let's get nearer civilization and send some word to the folks at home. They'll be getting worried."

"It doesn't seem as if there was a way out of here without using an airship," remarked Jackson.

But he and Tom finally reached the seldom-used road which ran along the field that contained the lonely shack, and, following this, they reached a farmhouse about a mile farther on. Greatly to their relief, there was a telephone in the place. True it was only a party line, set up by some neighboring farmers for their own private use, but one of the subscribers, to whose home the private line ran, had a long distance instrument, and after a talk with him, this man promised Tom to call up Mr. Swift and acquaint him with the fact that his son and Jackson were all right, and would be home later.

"And now," said Tom, after thanking their temporary host, a farmer named Bloise, "can you tell us anything about an old cabin that stands back there?" and he indicated the location of the mysterious shack.

"Well, yes, I can tell you a little about it, but not very much," said Mr. Bloise. "It was built, some years ago, by a rich New Yorker, who bought up a lot of land around here for a game preserve. But it didn't pan out. This cabin was only the start of what he was going to call a 'hunting lodge,' I believe it was. There was to be a big building on the same order, but it never was built.

"Some say the fellow lost all his money in Wall Street, and others say the state wouldn't let him make a game preserve here. However it was, the thing petered out, and the old shack hasn't been used since."

"Oh, yes, it has!" exclaimed Tom. "We just came from there, and there are signs which show some one has been sleeping there and eating there."

"There has!" exclaimed the farmer. "Well, I didn't know that."

"I did," said his son, a young man about Tom's age. "I meant to speak of it the other day. I saw an automobile turn into the old road that the men used when they built the shack. I thought it was kind of queer to see a touring car turn in there, and I meant to speak of it, but I forgot. Yes, some one has been at the old cabin lately."

"Do you know who they are?" asked Tom eagerly. "We are looking for a Mr. Nestor, who disappeared mysteriously about two weeks ago, and I just found his wallet there in the shack!"

"You did!" exclaimed Mr. Bloise. "That's queer! You relatives of this Mr. Nestor?" he asked.

"Not exactly," Tom answered. "Just very close friends."

"Well, it's too bad about his being missing in that way," went on the farmer. "I read about it in the paper, but I never suspected he was around here."

"Oh, we're not sure that he was," said Tom quickly. "Finding his wallet doesn't prove that," and he told the story of his own and Jackson's appearance on the scene, to the no small wonder of the farmer and his family. Tom said nothing about the finding of the files, nor the evidence he deduced from them. That was another matter to be taken up later.

"Who were in the auto you saw?" asked Tom of the farmer's son. "Was Mr. Nestor in the car?"

"I couldn't be sure of that. There were two men in the machine, and they were both strangers to me. They were talking together, pretty earnestly, it seemed to me."

"One did not appear as if he was being taken away against his will, did he?" asked Tom.

"No, I can't say that he did," was the answers "They looked to me, and acted like, business men looking over land, or something like that. They just turned in on the road that leads to the old hunting cabin, as we call it around here, and didn't pay any attention to me. Then I forgot all about them."

"Neither of them could have been Mr. Nestor," decided Tom. "At least it doesn't seem as if he'd talk at all companionably to a man who had treated him as we think Mr. Nestor has been treated. I guess that clew isn't going to amount to much."

"It may!" insisted Jackson. "They may have had Mr. Nestor

in the car all the while—concealed in the back you know. We've got to find out more about these men and their auto, Tom."

"Well, yes, perhaps we have. But how?"

"Station some one at the shack, or at the beginning of the private road. The men may come back."

"That's so—they may. We'll do that!" cried the young inventor. "We must tell the police and Mr. Nestor's folks what we have learned. How can we get back to Shopton in a hurry?" he asked the farmer.

"Well, I can drive you to the railroad station," was the answer.

"Thank you," remarked Tom. "We'll accept your offer. And as soon as we get back we must send some one from the shop to stand guard over the airship," he added in an aside to Jackson. "Those file fellows may come back."

"That's so, we can't take any chances."

The farmer soon had his team at the door, and, after they had had a hasty but satisfying supper at the farmhouse, the son drove Tom and Jackson several miles to a railroad station, where they could catch a train for Shopton.

In due season Tom's home was reached. He intended to stop but a minute, to assure his father that everything was all right, and then get out his speedy runabout to go to see Mary, to tell her the news.

But when Tom sought his father in the library, he was told that there was a visitor in the house.

"Tom," said his father, "this gentleman is from Washington. He wants to arrange for a government test of your silent airship. I told him I thought you were about ready for it."

"A government test!" cried Tom. "Why, I didn't think the government even knew I was working on such an idea!" Tom was greatly surprised.

CHAPTER XXIV

IN THE MOONLIGHT

With a reassuring smile the visitor from Washington looked at Tom Swift.

"The government officials," he said, "know more than some people give them credit for—especially in these war times. Our intelligence bureau and secret service has been much enlarged of late. But don't be alarmed, Mr. Swift," went on the caller, whose name was Mr. Blair Terrill. "Your secret is safe with the government, but I think the time is ripe to use it now—that is, if you have perfected it to a point where we can use it."

"Yes," answered Tom slowly, "the invention is practically finished and it is a success, except for a few minor matters that will not take long to complete.

"Our accident this afternoon had nothing to do with the efficiency of the silencer," Tom went on. "It was deliberately damaged by some spy. I'll take that up later. That I am interested to know how you heard of my Air Scout, as I call it."

"Well, we have agents, you know, watching all the inventors who have helped us in times past, and we haven't forgotten your giant cannon or big searchlight. I might say, to end your curiosity and lull your suspicions, that your friend, Ned Newton, who has been doing such good Liberty Bond work, informed us of your progress on the silent motor."

"Oh, so it was Ned!" exclaimed Tom.

"Yes. He told us the time was about ripe for us to make you an offer for your machine. I think we can use it to great advantage in scout work on the western front," went on the agent, and he soon convinced Tom that when it came to a knowledge of airships, he had some very pertinent facts at his disposal.

"When can you give me a test?" Mr. Terrill asked Tom.

"As soon as I can get my craft back to the shop and fit on a new outer case. That won't take long, as I have some spare ones. But I must help the Nestors," he went on, speaking to his father. "I didn't mention it over the wire," he added, "but we've found in the cabin a clew to the missing man. I must tell Mary and her mother, and help them all I can."

"And allow me to help, too," begged Mr. Terrill. "Since this affects you, Mr. Swift, and since you are, in a way, working for Uncle Sam, you must let him help you. This is the first I have heard of the missing gentleman, of whom your father just told me something, but you must allow me to help search for him. I will get the United States Secret Service at work."

"That will be fine!" cried Tom. "I wanted to get their aid, but I didn't see how I could, as I knew they were too busy with army matters and tracing seditious alien enemies, to bother with private cases. I'm sure the Secret Service men can get trace of the persons responsible for the detention of Mr. Nestor, wherever he is."

"They'll do their best," said Mr. Terrill. "I'm a member of that body," he went on, "and I'll give my personal attention to the matter."

Then followed a busy time. Tom did not get to bed until nearly morning. For he had to arrange to send some of his men to guard the stranded airship, and then he went to see Mary and her mother, taking them the good news that the search for Mr. Nestor would be prosecuted with unprecedented vigor.

"If it isn't too late!" sadly said the missing man's wife.

"Oh, I'm sure it isn't!" declared Tom.

In addition to sending a guard to the airship, other men, some of them hastily summoned from the nearest federal agency, were sent to keep watch in the vicinity of the lonely cabin. They had orders to arrest whoever approached, and a relay of the men was provided, so that watch could be kept up night and day. Besides this, other men from the Secret Service began scouring the country around the locality of the cabin, seeking a trace of the two persons the farmer's son had seen in the automobile.

"If Mr. Nestor is to be found, they'll find him!" declared Tom Swift.

Mr. Damon, as might be expected, was very much excited and wrought up over all these happenings.

"Bless my watch chain, Tom Swift!" cried the eccentric man, "but something is always happening to you. And to think I wasn't along when this latest happened!"

"Well, you can be in at the finish," promised Tom, and it was strange how his promise was fulfilled.

Meanwhile there was much to do. During the time the Secret Service men were busy looking up clews which might lead to the finding of Mr. Nestor and keeping watch in the vicinity of the hut, Tom had his airship brought back to the hangar, and a new silencer was attached. While this work was going on the place was guarded night and day by responsible men, so there was no chance for an enemy spy to get in and do further damage.

An investigation was made of the Universal Flying Machine Company, but nothing could be proved to link them with the outrage. Gale and Ware were in Europe—ostensibly on government business, but it was said that if anything could be proved connecting them with the attempt made on Tom Swift's craft, they would be deprived of all official contracts and punished.

All this took time, and the waits were wearisome, particularly in the case of Mr. Nestor. No further trace of him was found, though every effort was made. Tom began to feel that his boast of his enemies having to get up early in the morning to get ahead of him, had been premature, to say the least.

Tom Swift worked hard on his new Air Scout. He determined there would be nothing lacking when it came to the government test, and not only did he make sure that no enemy could tamper with his machine, but he took pains to see that no inherent defect would mar the test.

Jackson and the other men helped to the best of their ability, and Mr. Swift suggested some improvements which were incorporated in the new machine.

One of the puzzles the Secret Service men had to solve was that of the connection, if any, between the men who had to do with the missing Mr. Nestor and those who had damaged Tom's airship by filing the muffler case so it was weakened and burst. That there was some connection Tom was certain, but he could not work it out, nor, so far, had the government men.

At last the day came when the big government test was to be made. Tom had completed his Air Scout and had refined it to a point where even his critical judgment was satisfied. All that remained now was to give Mr. Terrill a chance to see how silently the big craft could fly, and to this end a flight was arranged.

Tom had put the silencer on a larger machine than the one he and Jackson had used. It held three easily, and, on a pinch, four could be carried. Tom's plan was to take Mr. Damon and Mr. Terrill, fly with them for some time in the air, and demonstrate how quiet his new craft was. Then, by contrast, a machine without the muffler and the new motor with its improved propellers would be flown, making as much noise as the usual craft did.

"I only wish," said Tom, as the time arrived for the official government test, "that Mary could be here to see it. She was the one who really started me on this idea, so to speak, as it was because I couldn't talk to her that I decided to get up a silent motor."

But Mary Nestor was too grief-stricken over her missing father to come to the test, which was to take place late one afternoon, starting from the aerodrome of the Swift plant.

"First," said Tom, to Mr. Terrill, "I'll show you how the machine works on the ground. I'll run the motor while the plane is held down by means of ropes and blocks. Then we'll go up in it."

"That suits me," said the agent. "If it does all you say it will do, and as much as I believe it will do, Uncle Sam will be your debtor, Mr. Swift."

"Well, we'll see," said Tom with a smile.

Preparations were made with the greatest care, and Tom went over every detail of the machine twice to make certain that, in spite of the precautions, no spy had done any hidden damage, that might be manifested at an inopportune moment. But everything seemed all right, and, finally, the motor was started, while Mr. Terrill, and some of his colleagues from the Army Aviation department looked on.

"Contact!" cried Tom, as Jackson indicated that the compression had been made.

The mechanic nodded, gave the big propeller blades a quarter turn and jumped back. In an instant the motor was operating, and the craft would have leaped forward and cleaved the air but for the holding ropes and blocks. Tom speeded the machinery up to almost the last notch, but those in the aerodrome hardly heard a sound. It was as though some great, silent dynamo were working.

"Fine!"

"Wonderful!"

"Wouldn't have believed it possible!"

These were some of the comments of the government inspectors.

"And now for the final test—that in the air," said Mr. Terrill.

Previous to this he and his colleagues had made a minute examination of the machinery, and had been shown the interior construction of the silencer by means of one built so that a sectional view could be had. Tom's principles were pronounced fundamental and simple.

"So simple, in fact, that it is a wonder no one thought of it before," said a navy aviation expert. "It is the last word in aircraft construction—a silent motor that will not apprise the enemy of its approach! You have done wonders, Mr. Swift!"

"I'd rather hear you say that after the air test," replied Tom, with a laugh. "Are you ready, Mr. Terrill?"

"Whenever you are."

"How about you, Mr. Damon?"

"Oh, I'm always ready to go with you, Tom Swift. Bless my trench helmet, but you can't sail any too soon for me!"

There was a genial laugh at his impetuosity, and the three took their seats in the big craft. Once more the engine was started. It operated as silently as before, and the first good impressions were confirmed. Even as the machine moved along the ground, just previous to taking flight into the air, there was no noise, save the slight crunch made by the wheels. This, of course, would be obviated when Silent Sam was aloft.

Up and up soared the great craft, with Tom at the engine and guide controls, while Mr. Terrill and Mr. Damon sat behind him, both eagerly watching. Mr. Terrill was there to find fault if he could, but he was glad he did not have to.

"The machine works perfectly, Mr. Swift," he said. "My report cannot be otherwise than favorable."

"We mustn't be in too much of a hurry," said Tom, who had learned caution some time ago. "I want to sail around for several hours. Sometimes a machine will work well at first, but defects will develop when it is overheated. I'm going to do my best to make a noise with this new motor."

But it seemed impossible. The machinery worked perfectly, and though Silent Sam took his passengers high and low, in big circles and small ones, there was no appreciable noise from the motor. The passengers could converse as easily, and with as little effort, as in a balloon.

"Of course that isn't the prime requisite," said Mr. Terrill, "but it is a good one. What we want is a machine that can sail over the enemy's lines at night without being heard, and I think this one will do it—in fact, I'm sure it will. Of course the ability of the passengers to converse and not have to use the uncertain tube is a great advantage."

As Tom Swift sailed on and on, it became evident that the test was going to be a success. The afternoon passed, and it began to grow dark, but a glorious full moon came up.

"Shall I take you down?" the young inventor asked Mr. Terrill.

"Not quite yet. I thoroughly enjoy this, and it isn't often I get a chance for a moonlight airship ride. Go a little lower, if you please, and we'll see if we attract any attention from the inhabitants of the earth. We'll see if they can possibly hear the machine, though I don't see how they can."

And they did not. Tom piloted the machine over Shopton, sailing directly over the center of the town, where there was a big crowd walking about. Though the airship sailed only a few hundred feet above their heads, not a person was aware of it, since the craft's lights were put out for this test.

"That settles it," said Mr. Terrill. "You have succeeded, Tom Swift!"

But Tom was not yet satisfied. He wanted a longer test. Hardly knowing why he did it he sent the craft in the direction of Mary Nestor's home. As he sailed across her lawn he saw, in the moonlight, that she and her mother were walking in the garden. They did not look up as the aircraft passed over their heads, and were totally unaware of its presence, unless they caught a glimpse of it as it flitted silently along, like some great bird of the night.

"It is perfectly wonderful!" declared Mr. Terrill, and he spoke in ordinary tones, that carried perfectly to the ears of Tom and Mr. Damon.

"Wonderful!" cried the eccentric man. "Bless my chimney, but it's the greatest invention in the world! Yes, it is! Don't tell me it 'isn't!"

And no one did.

Passing the Nestor home, the saddened occupants of which were unaware of the passage, Tom sent the Air Scout about in a circle, intending to proceed to the hangar. And then, some whim, perhaps, caused him to guide Silent Sam out toward the lonely hut. Mr. Damon and Mr. Tenrill seemed perfectly content to sail on and on indefinitely in the moonlight. Tom thought he would take them over a lonely neighborhood, and then bring them back.

In a little while the craft was directly over the stretch of country where the aeroplane accident had occurred, and where Tom and Jackson had found the deserted hut.

Rather idly Tom looked down, wondering if the Secret Service men were on the watch and if they had discovered anything.

Suddenly Tom was aware of an automobile moving along the field path toward the cabin. There were two men in the car, both on the front seat, and as Tom looked down the brilliant moonlight showed him the figure of another man, behind, and huddled in the tonneau of the car. The aeroplane was low enough for all these details to be seen by the moon's gleam, but the men in the car, not hearing any noise, did not look up, so they were unconscious of this aerial espionage.

"Look! Look!" exclaimed Tom in a low voice to his companions. "Doesn't that seem suspicious?"

CHAPTER XXV

THE GOLD TOOTH

Eagerly Mr. Damon and the government agent leaned over and looked down. In the moonlight they saw the same sight that had attracted Tom Swift. The touring car, the two men in front, and the huddled, bound figure in the back.

"Can you go down, Tom, without letting them hear you?" asked Mr. Damon, using a low voice, as if fearful the men in the automobile would hear him.

"I guess so," answered the young inventor. "I can land nearer to the cabin than Jackson and I did, and then we can see what these fellows are up to. It looks suspicious to me. That is, unless they're some of the Secret Service men, and have made a capture," he added to Mr. Terrill.

"Those aren't any of Uncle Sam's men," declared the agent. "That is, unless the bound one is. I can't see him very well. Better go down, and we'll see if we can surprise them."

"My plan," voiced Tom.

Quickly he shifted the rudder, and then, shutting off the motor, as he wanted to volplane down, he headed his craft for an open spot that showed in the bright moonlight. By this time the automobile and its occupants were out of sight behind a clump of trees, but Tom and his companions felt sure of the destination of the men—the deserted cabin in the wood.

As silently as a wisp of grass falling, the big craft came down on a level spot, and then, leaping out, the young inventor and his two companions crept along the path toward the cabin. Mr. Terrill was armed, Tom carried a flashlight, while Mr. Damon picked up a heavy club.

As soon as he came near a place where he thought the marks of the automobile wheels would show, Tom flashed his light.

"I thought so!" he exclaimed, as he saw the square, knobby tread marks left by the tires. "It's the same gang, or some of them in the same car. If we can only capture them!"

"The Secret Service men ought to do that," returned Mr. Terrill, but, as it developed later, they were not on hand, though through no fault of theirs.

On and on crept Tom and the two men, until they came within sight of the cabin. They saw a light gleaming in it, and Tom whispered:

"Now we have them! Work our way up quietly and make them surrender, if we find they're what we think."

"Is there a rear door?" asked Mr. Terrill in a whisper.

Tom answered in the negative, and then all three, in fan shape, crept up to the front portal. It was open, and silently reaching a place where they could make an observation, Tom and his companions looked in.

What they saw filled them with wild and righteous rage, and brought to an end the mystery of the disappearance of Mr. Nestor. For there he sat, bound in a chair, and at a table in front of him were two forbidding-looking men.

"What do you intend to do now?" asked Mr. Nestor in a faint voice. "I cannot stand this captivity much longer. You admit that you don't want me—that you never wanted me—so why do you keep me a prisoner? It cannot do the least good."

"There's no use going over that again!" exclaimed the harsh voice of one of the men. "We told you that if you will promise to keep still about what happened to you, and not to give the police any information about us, we'll let you go gladly. We don't want you. It was all a mistake, capturing you. You were the wrong man. But we're not going to let you go and have you set the police on us as soon as you get a chance. Give us your promise to say nothing, and we'll let you join your friends. If you don't—"

"Make no promises, Mr. Nestor!" cried Tom Swift in a ringing voice, as he leaped from his hiding place, followed by his companions. "Your friends are here, and you can tell them everything!"

"Up with 'em!" called Mr. Terrill to the two conspirators as he confronted them with his automatic pistol ready for firing. He had no need to mention hands—they knew what he meant and took the characteristic attitude.

"Tom! Tom Swift!" cried Mr. Nestor, struggling ineffectually at his bonds. "Is it really you?"

"Well, I hope it isn't any imitation," was the grim answer. "We'll tell you all about it later. Jove, but I'm glad we found you! If it hadn't been for Silent Sam we might never have been able to."

"Well, I don't know who Silent Sam is," said Mr. Nestor faintly. "But I'm sure I'm much obliged to him and your other friends. It has been very hard. Tell me, are my wife and Mary all right?"

"In good health, yes, but, of course, worrying," said Tom. "We saw them in the garden a little while ago. Now don't talk until I set you free."

And as Tom cut the ropes from Mr. Nestor, Mr. Damon used them to bind the two conspirators, while Mr. Terrill stood guard over them. And when they were safely bound, and

Mr. Nestor had somewhat recovered from the shock, Tom had a chance to examine the prisoners.

"What does it all mean? Who are you fellows, anyhow, and what's your game?" he demanded.

"Guess it—since you're so smart!" snapped one.

And no sooner had he opened his mouth and Tom had a glance of something gleaming brightly yellow, than the young inventor cried:

"The gold tooth! So it's you again, is it, you spy?"

The man shrugged his shoulders with an assumption of indifference. And, as Tom took a closer look, he became aware that the man was surely none other than Lydane, the spy he had chased into the mud puddle some weeks before. His companion was a stranger to Tom.

"What does it all mean, Mr. Nestor?" asked Tom. "Have these men held you a prisoner ever since you called for help on the moor that night?"

"Yes, Tom, they have. And I did call for help after they attacked me as I was riding my wheel, but I didn't know any one heard me. I began to be afraid no one would ever help me."

"We've been trying to, a long time," said Mr. Damon, "but we couldn't find you. Where did they keep you?"

"Here, part of the time," was Mr. Nestor's answer. "And in other lonely houses. They bound and gagged me when they took me from place to place."

"But what was their object?" asked Tom, concluding it was useless to question the two captives. "Why did they make you a prisoner, Mr. Nestor?"

"Because they took me for you, Tom."

"For me?"

"Yes. The night I called at your house, and found you were

not at home, I put back in my pocket a bundle of papers I had brought over to show you. They were plans of a little kitchen appliance a friend of mine had invented, and I wanted to ask your opinion of it."

"These scoundrels must have followed me, or have seen the bundle of papers, and, mistaking me for you, they followed, attacked me in a lonely spot and, bundling me and my wrecked wheel into an auto, carried me off. They first demanded that I gave up the 'plans,' and when I wouldn't they choked off my cries for help and knocked me into unconsciousness. Then they brought me here, and kept me here for several days.

"They soon learned that the plans I had weren't those they wanted, though what they were then after I couldn't imagine. Only, from what I later overheard, I knew they mistook me for you and that they were bitterly disappointed in not getting plans of some new airship you were working on. They have kept me a prisoner ever since, and though they offered to let me go if I would keep silent, I refused. I did not think, to secure my own comfort, I should let such men go unpunished if I could bring about their arrest."

"I should say not!" cried Tom.

"Did they treat you brutally, Mr. Nestor?" asked Mr. Damon.

"Not after they found out who I was, by looking through my wallet. Of course they didn't behave very decently, but they weren't actually cruel, except that they bound and gagged me. Oh, but I'm glad you came, Tom! How did it happen?"

Then they told Mr. Nestor their story, and how the test of the new Air Scout had led to his rescue.

"But where are the Secret Service men?" asked Mr. Terrill, when it became evident that none them was on guard at the cabin.

Later it developed that, by following a false clew, the Secret Service men had been drawn miles away from the cabin. And only that Tom and his companions in the silent airship saw the men. Mr. Nestor might not have been rescued for some further time.

His version of what had happened was correct. He had been mistaken for Tom, and the spy with the gold tooth and his accomplice had waylaid Mary's father, under the belief that it was Tom Swift with the plans of the new silent motor. Mr. Nestor had been attacked while riding his wheel in a lonely place, and had been carried off and kept in hiding, a prisoner even after his identity became known.

"Well, this is a good night's work!" exclaimed Tom, when the two rogues had been sent to jail and Mr. Nestor taken to the Bloise farmhouse, to be refreshed before he went home. Word of his rescue was telephoned to Mary and her mother, and it can be imagined how they regarded Tom Swift for his part in the affair.

Little the worse for his experience, save that he was very nervous, Mr. Nestor was taken home. He gave the details of his being waylaid, and told how the men, for many days, were at their wits' ends to keep him concealed when they found what a stir his disappearance had created. The conspirators were well supplied with money, and in the automobile they took their prisoner from one place to another. They had usurped the use of the cabin and had lived there nearly a week in hiding, leaving just before the first visit of Tom and Jackson. The rifled wallet had been dropped by accident.

And it did not take much delving to disclose the fact that, Lydane, "Gold Tooth," as he was called, and his crony, were spies in the pay of the Universal Flying Machine Company. As the men went under several aliases there is no need of giving their names. It is to be doubted if they ever used their real ones—or if they had any.

Of course, there was quite a sensation when Mr. Nestor was found, and a greater one when it became known the part the Universal Flying Machine people had in his disappearance in mistake for Tom. The officials of the company were indicted, and several of the minor ones sent to jail but Gale and Ware escaped by remaining abroad.

It came out that they both knew of the acts of Lydane and his companion in crime, and that the two officials realized the mistake that had been made by their clumsy operatives. It was believed that this knowledge led to the visit of Gale to Tom, the time the latter's suspicions were first aroused. Gale made a clumsy attempt to clear his own skirts of the conspiracy, but in vain, though he did escape his just punishment.

What had happened, in brief, was this. Gale and Ware, unable to secure Tom's services, even by the offer of a large sum of money, had stooped to the sending of spies to his shop, to get possession of information about his silent motor. This was after Gale had, by accident, heard Tom speaking of it to Mr. Damon.

But, thanks to Tom's vigilance, Bower was discovered. The man tripped into the mud hole lost in the muck the plans Bower passed to him. They were never recovered. Then Lydane tried again. He managed, through bribery, to gain access to the hangar where the new silent machine was kept, and, unable to get the silencer apart, tried to file it. In doing so he weakened it so that it burst.

The attempt to waylay Tom, and so get the plans from him, had been tried before this, only a mistake had been made, and

Mr. Nestor was caught instead. Finding out their error, Lydane and his companions did not tell the Universal people of their mistake, though Gale and Ware knew the attempt was to be made against Tom Swift.

Later, hearing that the young inventor was still at work on his invention, Gale was much surprised, and paid his queer visit, in an attempt to repudiate the actions of Lydane. At this time it was assumed that Gale and his partner did not know that it was Mr. Nestor who had been kidnapped by mistake or they might have insisted on his release. As it was, Lydane had Mary's father, and was afraid to let him go, though really their prisoner became a white elephant on the hands of the conspirators and kidnappers.

And it was after all this was cleared up, and Mr. Nestor restored to his family and friends, that one day, Tom Swift received another visit from Mr. Terrill, the government agent.

"Well, Mr. Swift," was the genial greeting, "I have come to tell you that the favorable report made by my friends and myself as to the performance of your noiseless motor, has been accepted by the War Department, and I have come to ask what your terms are. For how much will you sell your patent to the United States?"

Tom Swift arose.

"The United States hasn't money enough to buy my patent of a noiseless motor," he said.

"Wha—what!" faltered Mr. Terrill. "Why, I understood—you don't mean—they told me you were rather patriotic, and—"

"I hope I am patriotic!" interrupted Tom with a smile. "And when I say that the United States hasn't money enough to buy my latest invention I mean just that."

"My Air Scout is not for sale!"

"You mean," faltered the government agent. "You say—"

"I mean," went on Tom, "that Silent Sam is for Uncle Sam without one cent of cost! My father and I take great pleasure in presenting such machines as are already manufactured, those in process of making, and the entire patents, and all other rights, to the government for the winning of the war!"

"Oh!" said Mr. Terrill in rather a strange voice. "Oh!"

And that was all he could say for a little while.

But Tom Swift reckoned without a knowledge of a peculiar law which prohibits the United States from accepting gifts totally without compensation, and so, in due season, the young inventor received a check for the sum of one dollar in full payment for his silent motor, and the patent rights thereto. And Tom has that check framed, and hanging over his desk.

And so the silent motor became an accomplished fact and a great success. Those of you who have read of its work against the Boches, and how it helped Uncle Sam to gain the mastery of the sky, need not be reminded of this. By it many surprise attacks were made, and much valuable information was obtained that otherwise could not have been brought in.

One day, after the rogues had been sent to prison for long terms, and Tom had turned over to his government his silent aircraft—except one which he was induced to keep for his own personal use—the young inventor went to call on Mary Nestor. The object of his call, as I believe he stated it, was to see how Mr. Nestor was, but that, of course, was camouflage.

"Would you like to come for a ride, Mary, in the silent airship?" asked Tom, after he had paid his respects to Mr. Nestor and his wife. "We can talk very easily on board Silent Sam without the use of a speaking tube. Come on—we'll go for a moonlight sky ride."

"It sounds enticing," said Mary, with a shy look at Tom. "But wouldn't you just as soon sit on a bench in the garden? It's moonlight there, and we can talk, and—and—"

"I'd just as soon!" said Tom quickly.

And out they went into the beautiful moonlight; and here we will leave them and say good-bye.

THE END

Made in the USA
Middletown, DE
22 March 2024

51508643R00103